"Are you okay?"
The question he always asked, the one that melted her anxiety.

"I'm fine. Why?" But she knew, of course.

"I upset you."

She glanced around the glade, a pristine wilderness broken only by the train tracks.

"Only for a moment."

He eased an arm around her shoulders, let it lie there lightly as if gauging her acceptance. "You're safe with me."

"I know." And she did. In her head she knew. In her heart she knew. But bad experiences died hard.

When she didn't pull away, Austin drew her close to his side and she rested there, letting tension drain away. Gently he opened her fingers and touched the arrowhead, a gray gleam on her palm. "Quite a find. Rare and special. There aren't many left."

Like him. A rare and special find. A man to trust.

She was terrified of loving again, of taking a chance. If Austin knew everything about her past, would he reject her, as broken as she was?

Books by Linda Goodnight

Love Inspired

LINDA GOODNIGHT

Winner of a RITA® Award for excellence in inspirational fiction, Linda Goodnight has also won a Booksellers' Best Award, an ACFW Book of the Year award and a Reviewers' Choice Award from *RT Book Reviews*. Linda has appeared on the Christian bestseller list and her romance novels have been translated into more than a dozen languages. Active in orphan ministry, this former nurse and teacher enjoys writing fiction that carries a message of hope and light in a sometimes dark world. She and her husband, Gene, live in Oklahoma. Readers can write to her at linda@lindagoodnight.com or c/o Love Inspired Books, 233 Broadway, Suite 1001, New York, NY 10279.

Rancher's Refuge
Linda Goodnight

Love Inspired

Recycling programs
for this product may
not exist in your area.

TM LOVE INSPIRED BOOKS

ISBN-13: 978-0-373-81666-8

RANCHER'S REFUGE

www.LoveInspiredBooks.com

Printed in U.S.A.

Two are better than one....
If one falls down, the other can help him up.
But it is bad for the person who is alone and falls,
because no one is there to help.

—Ecclesiastes 4:9, 10

Prologue

Rumor says that if a prayer is murmured beneath Whisper Falls, God will hear and answer. Some folks think it's superstitious nonsense. Some think it's a clever ploy to attract tourists. Others believe that God works in mysterious ways, and prayers, no matter where whispered, are always heard.

Chapter One

Left hand riding lightly on his thigh, Austin Blackwell held the reins with the other and picked his way through the thick woods above Whisper Falls, Arkansas. If one more calf strayed into this no-man's land between his ranch and the cascading waterfall, he was putting up another fence. A really tall one. Barbed wire. Electrified. Let the folks of the small Ozark town whine and bellow that he was ruining the ambience or whatever they called the pristine beauty of these deep woods. They just didn't want to lose any tourist money. Well, he didn't want to lose any cattle money, either. So they were on even playing field. He'd never wanted to open the waterfall to tourism in the first place.

Now, every yahoo with an itch to climb down the rock wall cliff and duck behind the curtain of silvery water traipsed all over his property just to mutter a prayer or two. Wishful thinking or pure silliness. He'd made the trek a few times himself and he could guarantee prayers whispered there or anywhere else for that matter were a waste of good breath.

Something moved through the dense trees at his left and Austin pulled the horse to a stop. Cisco flicked his ears toward the movement, alert and ready to break after the maverick at the flinch of his master's knee.

"Easy," Austin murmured, patting the sleek brown neck while he scoped the woods, waiting for a sight or sound. Above him a squirrel chattered, getting ready for winter. Autumn leaves in reds and golds swirled down from the branches. Sunlight dappled between the trees, although the temperature was cool enough that Austin's jacket felt good.

He pressed his white Stetson tighter and urged the bay onward in the direction of the falls, the direction from which the movement had come. Might be the maverick.

"Coyote, probably." But black bear and cougar weren't out of the question. He tapped the rifle holster, confident he could handle anything he encountered in the woods. Outside the ranch was a different matter.

The roar of the falls increased as he rode closer. Something moved again and he twisted in the sad-

dle to see the stray heifer break from the opposite direction. Cisco responded with the training
of a good cutting horse. Austin grappled for the
lariat rope as the calf split to the right and crashed
through the woods to disappear down a draw.

Cisco wisely put on the brakes and waited for
instructions. Austin lowered the rope, mouth
twisting in frustration. No use endangering a
good horse in this rugged, uneven terrain.

At least the stray had headed in the right direction, back toward the ranch.

"Yep, I'm puttin' up another fence." He patted
Cisco's neck with a leather-gloved hand. Somewhere along the meager stretch of old barbed
wire the calves had found a place to slip through.
Maybe in one of the low places or through a wash-
out from one of the many creeks branching from
the Blackberry River. Finding the break across
three miles of snaggy underbrush would be a chal-
lenge.

But Austin liked it up here on the grassy, leaf-
and hickory-lined ridge above Whisper Falls.
Always had, especially before the stories started
and people came with their noise and tents and
plastic water bottles. Before the name changed
from Millerville to Whisper Falls—a town council decision to attract tourists. He understood. He
really did. Ruggedly beautiful, this area of the
Ozarks was isolated. Transportation was poor and

there was little opportunity for economic growth, especially since the pumpkin cannery shut down.

The remoteness was why he'd come here. The economy was why he ranched.

Those were also the reasons the little town had changed its name and started the ridiculous marketing campaign to attract tourism. Whisper Falls. Austin snorted. No amount of marketing moved God to answer prayers.

He shifted in the saddle to look toward the ninety-feet-high waterfall.

Here, the Blackberry River tumbled faster than near the ranch, picking up speed before plummeting over the cliff in a white, foamy, spectacular display of nature's force and beauty.

The solitude of the woods soothed him, helped him forget. Nature didn't judge the way people would. He could be himself. He could relax.

The air was clean here, too, tinted with the spray of freshness from the bubbling falls. It almost made him feel clean inside again. Almost. He breathed the crispness into his lungs, held the scent. Hickory and river, moist earth and rotting leaves. Good smells to an outdoorsman. Great smells to a man whose past stank like sewage.

"Better get moving, Cisco. Maybe we can find the fence break before dark."

He pulled the bay around and that's when he saw the woman. A slim figure in dark slacks and bright blue sweater moved quickly from tree to tree in some game of hide-and-seek. Curious, Austin took out his field glasses to look around, expecting a child or lover to join the game. No one did.

Austin swung the binoculars back to the woman. What he saw spurred him to action.

Annalisa Keller stifled a sob. She had to hide. She had to get away. "Please, God. Help."

She heard him coming, thrashing, crashing through the dry leaves and underbrush like the madman he was. Knees rattling, she cradled her left arm and stumbled down the rocky incline. Straight ahead, the falls roared, a rush of sound with the power to sweep her away. The thought tempted, beckoned. Jump in and be swept away. He could never find her. No one would.

Teeth chattering, she resisted the frightening urge. The instinct to survive was too strong. She couldn't give up now.

"Help me, God," she whispered again, grappling to the sides of slick rock, edging closer to the beckoning water, to the screaming falls. The footpath was worn and well-used, as if others had come this way before her. She followed the stones, clinging with cold fingers to the jutting rocks as she edged along the cliff face, hoping to hide from searching eyes above.

The roar of the falls grew louder still. Her heart thundered in answer. Before her was the waterfall. Behind her was the direction she'd come. An awful thought engulfed her. Why had she begun the descent to the falls? If he spotted her, she'd be trapped between him and the raging water.

But she knew why. She'd been running blindly with no destination in mind other than escape.

She sensed him coming, felt the air change with another presence. In desperation, Annalisa moved forward, praying there was sanctuary against the wet cliff face. One more step and...

The world went silent. A deafening silence.

Shocked, Annalisa wondered for one beat if she'd actually jumped into the foaming pool below the waterfall, if she was dead.

Trembling, she reached out, touched the silver curtain of water in front of her. A hard rain shower soaked her hand, cold and prickly like needles of ice.

In awe, she glanced to each side and then upward. The sight was dizzying. Behind was solid rock, wet and slick and shiny, with a jutting overhang high above. Water rocketed over the cliff with such force that a quiet space, like a white-noise machine, formed behind the cascade. She stood on a two-foot ledge, protected in the back by a wall of rock and hidden in front by the waterfall.

It was like something out of the movie *The Last of the Mohicans*.

Her shoulders relaxed a tiny bit. Maybe James hadn't seen her descend. Maybe he wouldn't know she was here. Warmth oozed from her nose. Swiping at the liquid with the back of her hand, Annalisa came away with blood. She shivered, both from cold and shock.

James had nearly killed her this time. He'd kicked her out of the car, tried to run her down and then driven away. She'd seen him angry plenty of times, but never like this. Never so completely out of control.

With a shaky sigh, she closed her eyes and leaned her head against the hard, damp rocks at her back. Her arm ached all the way to her wrenched shoulder. She wondered if the bone was broken.

Never again. Never, never again. She'd said that the first time he'd hurt her, but this time she meant it.

She listened, intent, but could hear nothing from within the watery cocoon.

Maybe James hadn't followed her. Maybe he would go home to California without her. He'd said she wasn't worth the headache. But she also knew his terrible egotistical pride. James got what James wanted. He hated being the loser.

A scrambling noise jerked her to attention. A rock clattered against rock.

Annalisa's heart jacked into overdrive. Blood pounded in her ears. If he'd found her, she was as good as dead, a casualty to the rocky pool below. No one would ever know he'd pushed her.

For a second she was helpless. Then the need to survive kicked in. He would not take her down easily.

With her one good hand, she groped the space at her feet and found what she needed. A rock. A small one, but a weapon just the same.

The sound of movement increased, grew closer. A shadow moved. A big shadow.

Shaking hard, she raised her arm.

A hulk ducked behind the curtain of water. Annalisa's heart hammered wildly. She braced to defend.

"Hey, lady, are you ok—"

With a sob, she struck, crashing the rock down with all her ebbing strength.

"Hey!" The shadow staggered back, arm upraised in defense.

The haze of fear cleared from Annalisa's eyes. A man had joined her behind the falls but not James. He wasn't James. He was a big, dark, angry stranger in a cowboy hat.

And she'd bashed him with a rock.

* * *

Austin blinked rapidly at the slender woman with the stunned face. She was as pale as strained milk and bleeding from the nose and mouth.

"What's going on here?"

She dropped her whamming rock and shrunk away from him.

Austin frowned. Why the heck was she cowering?

"I'm sorry. I thought—" She clamped her pale, chattering lips shut.

He rubbed at the growing knot at his temple, surprised to find his hat barely askew. As he adjusted the Stetson, the stars subsided enough that he could remember why he'd come down from the ridge to begin with. "What happened to your face?"

She shook her head. Hair as gold as a palomino horse clung to the sides of her face. It was a good face, nice bone structure, with long blue eyes that took up a lot of physical real estate. But her nose was bleeding and her upper lip puffed out like a bee sting.

Those eyes shifted to one side. In a low murmur she said, "I fell."

"Here? On the rocks? Did you fall from the ridge?"

"Um, yes. On the rocks. I was...um...hiking." Again, her eyes skittered all over the place. Everywhere but on him. Austin's sixth sense crackled like milk-drenched Rice Krispies. There was something the little lady wasn't saying. His gaze dropped to her shoes. Heels. Strappy, spiky heels. She was hiking in those?

"Looks like you need a doc. Can I call someone for you?" He fished in his pocket and dragged out a cell. "No guarantee of service up here."

She shook her head. "There's none. I tried."

Other than his, Austin didn't see a cell phone. In fact, she carried nothing at all, and unless his eyesight had worsened in the past three minutes, she had no pockets in the sleek pants and fitted sweater. The sixth sense squealed louder. Something was amiss.

He glanced at his trusty little flip phone. The woman was right. The satellite logo was spinning like a top and coming up short. No service. "You hiking up here alone?"

"What?" She looked startled, doe-eyed and guilty about something. A drop of blood rimmed one nostril. She dabbed it with a wrist.

"You said you were hiking and fell. You alone?"

"Oh. Um…yes. Alone." Again the shifty eyes, the jittery movements. Add a hard swallow for measure and he was sure the lady was lying through her even, white teeth.

She started to move as if to pass him. Austin stepped back but not in time. She bumped the rock face. A cry slipped from swollen lips as she grabbed for her left arm. "Oh, God, please."

Austin jacked an eyebrow. Was she one of those fruitcakes lured by the town's "rumor" of answered prayers? "Forget it. It's just a story made up to draw tourists."

She blinked, cradling the arm against her chest. "I don't know what you mean."

"Praying under the waterfall." He motioned toward the foaming spray of water. "Useless."

With a bewildered look, she doubled forward and moaned. Her body shook like a motherless calf on Christmas morning.

Against his better judgment, Austin accepted what he had to do. "That's it. You're going to a doctor."

"I think my arm may be broken, but…" She ended on a sob.

"But what?"

Her pale lips tightened beneath worried eyes. Austin huffed a frustrated sigh. One, the woman was hurt. Two, she was lying. Three, he wasn't sure what else to do.

He didn't like getting involved in other people's business. In fact, he didn't like getting involved with any kind of people for any reason, but he wasn't a heartless mule, either, who'd leave a woman with a broken arm five miles from the nearest working telephone.

"Come on." He edged his way from beneath the falls and out into the perfect early autumn day. Or it had been perfect until the calf disappeared and a woman showed up.

Austin started up the rocks toward his waiting horse before he remembered. The woman had only one good arm. Going down to the falls was an adventure. Getting back up required two good hands and a stout disposition. With a sigh, he pivoted, taking care on the slick limestone.

Wet and shaking, the blonde edged cautiously along the wall, still cradling the arm.

He trudged back to her. "How did you get down here anyway?"

She shrugged but said nothing. Her silence bothered him.

"Oh, right, you fell." *And I flew in on a Learjet.* "Come on. You first." If she slipped, he could catch her.

She skittered past him, huddled into herself, the bright blue sweater stretched taut across her stooped back. She was like a wounded blue jay, a flash of color against the deep gray rocks.

Austin wanted to take hold of her elbow to steady her ascent but she didn't give him the chance. She was a strange creature, a mystery with her scared-doe eyes and defiant rock thumping.

He lifted a hand to his temple, found the knot.

It didn't hurt much, nothing compared to how the woman's arm must feel. He'd had a broken bone once when a horse and cow collided and his leg was sandwiched between. Hurt like the dickens.

He could hear her breathing, the puffs of someone unaccustomed to long hikes on rough terrain. He thought of her girly heeled shoes, her upscale clothes, the bleeding face. She was lying.

The question was, why?

He moved in behind her and took her elbow with one hand and supported her back with the other. She flinched, a motion that made Austin grind his back teeth. But she didn't pull away, a good thing, because Austin was a stubborn man. If he had to, he'd swoop her over one shoulder and cart her up the rise like a sack of sweet feed. She probably didn't weigh much more than a hundred-pound sack of oats.

They reached the top of the ridge and she paused for a moment to catch her breath and look around. Not a casual glance at nature's beauty, but a search. A furtive, wary search.

For what?

Austin's eyes narrowed. "My horse is this way."

She spun toward him. "Horse?"

"Look, lady, there are no roads back in here. The nearest ATV trail is three miles and then it's another two miles to town. You either walk or ride horses." Or like some high-rollers, you flew over in helicopters. Man, did that ever set his teeth on edge. He scowled. "You didn't fly in on a helicopter, did you?"

"No." She hitched her chin. He noticed long red marks on her throat. Funny place to be injured in a fall. "I can walk if you'll lead the way."

Stacking fists on hips, Austin rolled his eyes. "Afraid of horses?"

"No."

"Then why walk when you can ride?"

"But you said…it's your horse."

"I don't know where you come from, lady, but around here a man doesn't ride while the woman walks. What's your name anyway?"

She hesitated before saying, "Annalisa."

No last name. Interesting.

"Fancy name." But then she was a fancy-looking woman, sleek and well-groomed. Except for the blood and bruises. "I'm Austin Blackwell. You're on my ranch." Practically.

She pressed her lips together in an expression of worry. "I'm sorry."

He glared at her. "For what?"

Her fingers fluttered. Exactly like the pulse above her collarbone. "Trespassing. I should have asked before…uh…hiking."

Austin pinned her with a look. "Yeah. Hiking."

It was none of his business if she fell or jumped

or was attacked by Sasquatch, just as it was none of his business if she lied. None.

Austin started to sweat.

The last thing he needed was a woman with suspicious injuries.

They approached Cisco who'd found a patch of grass to nibble on. The sooner he got Miss Annalisa mystery woman off this mountain and into someone else's care, the easier he could breath.

"You know how to mount? One foot in the stirrup. Throw the other over. I'll give you a boost. You take care of the arm."

She nodded and with a gritty determination given her condition, stuck a foot in the stirrup and hopped. Austin leaned in to help, a hand beneath her free foot, the other ready to brace her back. The scent of perfume, definitely not the cheap stuff, but mysterious like her, contrasted with the earthy, wetness of the falls. He did his best not to notice, but the fragrance reminded him of something. Something he'd put out of his mind long ago.

He clenched his teeth against the fantasy, hoisted her other foot and put her into the saddle as gently as possible. She was light if leggy, tall enough to reach his stirrups. And he was no small fry.

Annalisa's face paled with the movement. She bit back a groan. A small one, but he heard it.

"Easy," he said, feeling like a heartless slug for hurting her. If he wouldn't have been thinking of her long legs and heady scent, he could have been more careful.

Yeah, and if that sorry calf hadn't gotten out, he wouldn't be here in the first place with his sixth sense screaming like a banshee.

Ifs didn't mean much in Austin's vocabulary. If life was as it should be, he'd still be in Texas.

He took Cisco's reins and tossed them over the saddle horn. In quick, efficient movements he swung into the saddle in front of his guest, taking care not to jar her. Annalisa leaned back, away from contact.

Austin shifted in the saddle to look at her. "Brace your bad arm against my back and give me your other."

She hesitated, clearly not wanting to touch him. Well, too stinkin' bad. He didn't want her falling off.

"One broken arm is enough," he barked. She flinched, eyes widening.

He grabbed her good hand and slapped it against his rib cage. With a *tsk* and slight tightening of his knees, he set Cisco on an easy walk through the trees.

Behind him, Annalisa was as stiff as new leather.

What was up with this lady?

Chapter Two

Annalisa curled her fingers into the rough brown duck of the cowboy's jacket, lips stiff from trying to stifle the moans of pain. Jostling on the back of a horse wasn't helping her arm or any of the other places she hurt.

Austin Blackwell frightened her with his dark scowls and sharply barked words, although he didn't seem the violent type. But neither had James when they'd first started dating.

She darted a quick look around, nerves jittery. The forest was gorgeous, a tapestry of rich color and scent, flush with autumn sun. If she'd not been in pain and wasn't constantly on the alert for James, she could have enjoyed the ride.

When was the last time she'd been on a horse?

The animal—Cisco, he'd called the bay—had a smooth stride, his muscular body easily handling two passengers. She wasn't sure where they were headed, but the horse knew.

"Is this the way to the hospital?"

The cowboy tilted his white hat forward as if signaling something up ahead. "We'll take my truck."

They crested a rise and then started down an incline into a small valley. In the center of clear pasture land, with no other houses around, sat a long, low ranch-style house and a number of outbuildings. Three dogs bolted from the porch, tails wagging, barking a chorus of excited welcome. There was a black lab, some kind of big shaggy shepherd with white eyebrows and...an apricot poodle?

"Shut up!"

Annalisa tensed at the cowboy's command. He twisted toward her. "Not you. Them."

She *knew* that, and yet she'd jumped.

They rode directly to the porch, a structure that ran the length of the red brick house and was railed by rough cedar. A broom leaned against the railing. Someone had planted a big pot of yellow mums next to the door. Annalisa eyed the cowboy. His wife, perhaps?

With the quick, lithe movements she'd noted before, he dismounted and then lifted her easily to the ground. He was big and gruff, but his touch was deceivingly gentle. She'd yet to categorize him other than cowboy. Faded jeans, brown duck jacket and a white hat. And of course, the horse. She had the ridiculous thought that good guys wear white hats. Ridiculous indeed, considering her poor ability to judge men.

Austin Blackwell. Nice name for a cowboy. A pretty big guy with shoulders wide enough to handle a calf, he was around her age. From riding at his back, she knew that he was solid muscle.

She shivered. A big, dangerous man who'd been none too happy about finding her on his land. She slid a subtle glance toward him. He'd started toward the porch, only to be met by the dog trio.

The three groveled around his boots, and the white-browed shepherd bared its teeth in a comical smile of welcome while the poodle pranced on hind legs in a dance of joy. In spite of her throbbing arm, Annalisa smiled, too. Austin dropped a work-gloved hand to the highest head and scratched while the other two butted up against his legs, waiting their turn.

"Truck's there." He motioned toward the side of the house to a truck shed. Under an awning sat a white late-model Ford with big wheels flecked with mud. "I'll grab the keys and we'll go see the doc."

He tromped up the steps, taking a minute to stomp his boots on a black welcome mat before disappearing inside.

Panic welled in Annalisa's throat, a knot she couldn't swallow. She was suddenly aware of how much the cowboy's presence eased her anxiety. Now, alone in the open yard, terror rushed in.

Pulse tripping wildly, her breath quickened as she hurried to the white truck and tried the side door. It was unlocked. She clambered inside, slammed the door and slapped at the lock with shaky fingers. Still, her heart raced as wildly as if she'd run all the way from the waterfall.

She leaned her head against the tall seat, shut her eyes and breathed in the scent of new leather from an air freshener dangling from the rearview mirror. "Lord, if you'll help me find a way out of this mess, I promise—"

The driver's door opened. Annalisa spun toward the sound. The movement sent shock waves from her shoulder to her wrist. Instinctively she curled inward and grimaced.

"Easy." The cowboy's light green gaze steadied her.

Before he could step up into the driver's seat, the apricot poodle jumped onto the long bench beneath the steering column.

"Get down, you wiggling wad of Brillo." Face stern, Austin moved to one side and pointed toward the ground. Even though the poodle withered in dejection, her little fuzzy tail worked overtime. The cowboy's voice gentled. "Go on, Tootsie. Get down. You can't go this time."

Resigned, the dog obeyed. On the way out, the "Brillo pad" lifted up on her hind legs to swipe a tongue across Austin's face. The cowboy grunted, shaking his head as he climbed into the truck. Annalisa was almost sure the corners of his mouth quivered with affection.

Keys rattled and the truck engine roared to life. Austin adjusted the shifter, but as they backed out of the carport, a dark green Nissan whipped into the driveway and stopped. A woman in blue scrubs with a curly black ponytail strode toward Austin's side of the truck.

Curiosity curled in Annalisa's belly. Was this the wife?

Austin lowered his window. With a jerk of his chin toward Annalisa he said, "Found this lady at the falls. I'm taking her to see Dr. Ron."

The woman narrowed moss green eyes at Annalisa. "What happened?"

"I fell." The lie was easier this time.

"The mountain trails are good for that. Anything I can do?" The last question was for Austin.

"You can cook something."

"So can you." The woman laughed, dimples flashing in a longish face. "I was asking if there is anything I can do for her." She stuck her head through the window, stretching past Austin. "By

the way, I'm Cassie. My big brother has no social skills."

An odd trickle of interest shifted over Annalisa
as she introduced herself to Cassie. The sister,
not the wife.

"Are you a nurse?"

Teeth flashed as Cassie laughed. "A hairdresser,
but I know a bum arm when I see one. You need
an X-ray. By the way, you have great hair. I'd love
to get my hands on it."

Annalisa's fingers flew to the dark blond mass
of thick, shoulder-length waves. Inwardly she smirked
at the vain reaction. Even an injury didn't stop
a woman from enjoying a compliment. "Thank
you."

Cassie tapped Austin on the shoulder with a
fist. "Get going. She's in a lot of pain." By now the
three dogs were hopping around the sister. "Bring
us a pizza. I'm in no mood to cook."

Austin groaned. "You brought pizza last night."

"So I like pizza."

"And hate to cook."

Cassie picked up the poodle and waved his paw.
"Burgers, then. With fries and pies. Apple."

Austin didn't argue. He put the gear in Reverse
and headed away from the ranch.

"How far?"

"To the doc's?" He glanced toward her and back
to the bumpy gravel road. "About ten minutes."

With an acknowledging nod, Annalisa braced her arm against her chest, leaned back against the headrest and prayed that James had gone on without her.

Austin whipped the truck into the parking spot marked "Physicians Only" and killed the motor in front of Johnson's Medical Clinic. Dr. Ron Johnson's maroon Jeep was in the lot and he was the only physician for twenty-five miles. Austin figured the two extra physician parking spots outside the office were wishful thinking on the part of the overzealous town council.

The town was like that these days, optimistic in the face of a lousy economy. Mayor Fairchild, whom everyone called Rusty, had asked the churches to pray, a request that had a handful of folks up in arms over the separation of church and state issue. Austin figured praying didn't hurt anything. It just didn't help.

He hustled around the truck to open the door for Annalisa, something she was already struggling to do on her own. He helped her out and led the way up on the sidewalk and into the small, modern clinic. Inside, the usual scent of antiseptic cooled the air.

At the receptionist's window, Austin jerked a thumb toward Annalisa. "Got an injured woman here. Dr. Ron available?"

"I'll tell him, Austin. You all sit down and fill out this mess of papers." She stuck a clipboard across the divider. "I'll only be a jiff."

"Thanks, Wilma."

Austin handed the clipboard to Annalisa along with a pen, but his restlessness wouldn't let him sit in one of the brown vinyl chairs. Coming into town was not a favorite activity, and usually when he did, he kept to the basics—the Farm and Ranch Store, groceries, gas. An injured woman raised suspicions, and he did not want anyone asking questions.

True to her word, the bun-haired Wilma returned in a jiff to motion them toward an exam room. Dr. Ron waited inside, drying his hands on paper towels. Close to forty, the doc looked half that because of his boyish freckles and the cowlick torturing his sandy hair. He tossed the towels in a levered can and gestured to the exam table.

"Who's sick?" One quick look at Annalisa and then the chart Wilma poked at him and he said, "Never mind. What happened?"

Annalisa cast a troubled glance at Austin. "I fell."

Austin saw the worry hanging on her like a baggy shirt. She knew he didn't believe her story and probably wanted him gone. Which he should be. Feeling a little chagrined to have followed a stranger into an exam room in the first place, he said, "I'll wait outside, but I want to talk to the doc when you're done."

Dr. Ron met his gaze and nodded. "Sure thing. Now young lady, you hop right up here and let's have a look at that arm."

Austin heard the latter as he exited the room. There was a lot Annalisa wasn't saying. Even though it was none of his business, Austin figured the doc should know his suspicions.

He folded his arms across his chest and leaned against the wall beside the door. Wilma whipped past, leading the way for a woman and a flush-faced, coughing child. Austin figured if a man stood here all day he'd catch every disease known to medicine.

A few minutes later, the wooden door swung open and Dr. Ron sent Annalisa down the hall with an assistant for an X-ray. Austin joined the doctor inside the exam room and shut the door.

"I think she's lying," he blurted.

Water sprayed as Dr. Ron washed his hands yet again in the strong-scented soap. "How did you get involved?"

Austin's gut tightened. Was the doc accusing him of something? "I found her."

A freckled eyebrow lifted. "You don't know her? She's not a friend or relative?"

Anxiety pushed from Austin's gut to his throat. When he'd brought her here, he hadn't been thinking clearly. He'd never considered that someone might point a finger at him. He rolled the brim of his hat between nervous fingers. "Never saw her before today. She was at Whisper Falls. Or rather under it."

"Praying?" The doc's lips twitched, but the humor didn't reach his serious blue eyes.

"Probably. She was running from something or someone. She claims she was hiking, but I don't believe her. Take a look at her shoes and clothes."

"Could she have fallen while traipsing over the falls to pray?"

Austin barked a sarcastic laugh. "Did you notice the red marks on her throat?"

The doc raised both eyebrows in insult. The cowlick quivered. "If I hadn't I should find another occupation."

"What are you going to do about it?"

Dr. Ron spread his palms. "Nothing I can do. She's a grown woman, not a child. If she says she fell, I have to take her word for it. She might be telling the truth, although like you, I don't think the bruises came from a tumble on the rocks. The broken arm, however, very well may have."

"Maybe." Austin patted his hat impatiently against his leg. Dr. Ron was a good sort. He'd treated Austin when a horse stumbled with him, and he'd stitched him up a couple of times. He was trustworthy. "She's scared of something,

Doc. Jumpy as a grasshopper. I think someone hurts her."

Dr. Ron pressed his freckled lips together in silent consideration before saying, "I'll push a little harder for details, Austin, but if she wants to keep the whole truth to herself, I can't force it out of her."

At that moment, Wilma and Annalisa came out of the X-ray room and headed toward them.

Knowing the doc was right didn't make Austin like the answer any better. Grumbling under his breath, he slapped his hat against his leg. "I'll be in the waiting room."

Annalisa sat perfectly still while the doctor wound wet cast material from her wrist to her biceps.

"Wear this for three weeks and then you get the grand prize," the amiable doctor said, "a shorter waterproof version of this dandy little number."

She stared dubiously at her forearm, frozen at a right angle. "When will I be able to move my elbow?"

"After this one comes off. Fortunately all the bones are aligned or you'd be on your way to Hot Springs to an orthopedist. All we have to do is keep the bone as still as possible for it to heal properly, and you should be as good as new."

She shuddered at the memory of James's strong

hands and the loud pop as he intentionally rotated her arm until she screamed. The gleam in his eyes, the bulging veins in his neck. The fury.

She squeezed her eyes tight, scared just thinking about him. *God, I never want to see James Winchell again. Show me what to do.*

Dr. Ron's gentle voice jerked her to attention. "I'm a doctor, Miss Keller. Anything you tell me is confidential. If you need help…"

He let the offer dangle while he completed the wrap and pressed his palms against the drying cast. Heat penetrated through the padding.

The doctor knew she hadn't fallen, or at least he suspected.

She wanted to tell someone about the abuse, but shame held her back. Shame and the knowledge that she was responsible. She'd broken off the relationship once and been foolish enough to let James back into her life. She'd believed his promises and accepted his explanations. He was under stress at work. She'd provoked him. It wouldn't happen again.

But it had.

Annalisa lowered her lashes. "Thank you, but I'll be fine."

Dr. Ron was silent for a couple of beats while he scribbled on her chart.

"Wilma will have some instructions for you on cast care and problems to look out for." He ripped a piece of paper from a pad and handed her a prescription. "Austin will take you by the pharmacy to get this pain medicine filled. Take one if you need it, every four hours for pain. Nights are usually the worst."

"Thank you, Doctor." Annalisa slid off the slick, paper-covered table and went to the door.

"Call if you need anything," he said, serious eyes boring into her as if he knew everything she'd been through. "Anything at all."

Annalisa understood his implication. With a nod, she hurried out.

In the waiting room, the cowboy sat scrunched in a chair, one boot crossed over the opposite knee and his pale green gaze glued to the hall leading to the exam rooms.

When he spotted her, he unfolded his length from the small chair and stood. An imposing man, he was tall, and dark as a thundercloud with shoulders as wide as a quarterback's.

One look at her casted arm and his mouth curved. "Lime green?"

From somewhere she found an answering smile and lifted the cast higher. It weighed a ton. "I'm a fashion diva."

"Yeah, we get a lot of calls for those in Whisper Falls," he said wryly, and she wasn't sure if he joked or not. "Where to from here?"

She held out the prescription, feeling like a

bum. She'd imposed on this man enough, but what else could she do? This wasn't exactly familiar terrain. "Do you know where a pharmacy is?"

"Not *a* pharmacy. *The* pharmacy. Jessup's. Like Dr. Ron's clinic, the only one in town."

Annalisa followed broad shoulders to his truck, grateful that this man had been the one to find her in the woods. A little taciturn, he was a take-charge kind of guy who saw what needed doing and did it. Maybe she should worry about that, but right now, she had no choice except gratitude.

As she got into his truck for the second time that day, a troubling thought struck her.

"Oh, no," she breathed, fingers pressed to her lips in dismay.

"What?" Austin hooked an arm over the steering wheel and shifted in her direction.

"I can't fill the prescription." She swallowed, gut fluttering with a new anxiety. Her situation had just become more dire.

Black eyebrows dipped. "Why not?"

"I—I must have lost my handbag when I fell." A total lie. James had her purse in his car. When he'd shoved her out, she'd had no time to grab anything. Her phone, her money, her ID. Everything was in her purse. In time she could replace most of it, but that didn't get her beyond this very awkward moment.

"You're saying you don't have any money?"

A flush of heat rushed up her neck and burned her cheeks. "Not at the moment. I have money back in…at home. Just not with me."

Intelligent and already suspicious, he jumped on her slip of the tongue. "Back where, Annalisa? You're not from Whisper Falls, so where's your car? Where's your hiking gear? People don't just drop out of the sky and start hiking through miles of woods and hills to a waterfall in sissy shoes like that." He gave her feet a scathing glare.

Acid burned in her stomach. Like the doctor, the cowboy was no fool, and her story *was* as thin as nylon.

"Forget the prescription. I've been too much bother already. Please, just take me to the nearest hotel."

"How you gonna pay for *that?*"

She opened her mouth, only to shut it again. How indeed? The receptionist at the doctor's office had taken her insurance information on nothing but faith in her promise to scan and send the card at a later date. She doubted a hotel would be as forgiving.

"I don't know." She pressed a hand to the dull headache drumming at her temples. "I'll think of something. Let me think a minute."

The cowboy apparently hadn't a minute to spare because he started the engine and aimed the truck down the narrow, curving street. She had no idea where they were going and at the moment, didn't care. She was stuck in the rural Ozarks without a dime or a credit card or a checkbook. And calling James to retrieve those items was out of the question.

She would rather live under that waterfall for the rest of her life and eat bugs.

Annalisa leaned her throbbing, hot head against the side window. Her whole face ached and she wondered if bruises were starting to appear. James was usually more careful. A slap here or there or cold intimidation, but not all-out battering.

She shivered and pressed closer to the door. An angry man was a powerful thing. And no matter how hard she'd tried, she'd not been always been able to pacify James.

Annalisa vowed not to make Austin Blackwell angry.

With a furtive glimpse at his dark, solemn profile, she wondered if she already had.

She'd gotten herself in this predicament. Now what? She could use her phone-a-friend option, but her friends were also James's. They all considered him the catch of the day. Somewhere in their eight-month dating history, he'd steered her toward people in his circle and away from hers.

Unshed tears pushed at the back of her eyelids. If she had a family to rely on. If she wasn't so terribly alone. If she hadn't made such a mess of things.

Regrets. So very many regrets. What a fool she'd been to bend to James's every whim, even to the point of drifting away from her church. *God, forgive me.*

Shame was an ugly companion.

Holding back frustrated tears, she focused on the streets of Whisper Falls and tried to think of anything but her predicament. The town was small with only a long strip of businesses on either side of about five blocks. The buildings were old, probably turn of the last century, and many had been renovated into darling shops. In other circumstances, she would have explored Auntie's Antiques, Sweets and Eats, the old brick train station. A spired courthouse with a long pillared porch was fronted by the statue of a soldier and a tall granite memorial to Vietnam vets. The list of names engraved on the onyx plaque both stunned and saddened her. Whisper Falls may be small, but it had given of its best.

Some of the buildings were run-down, but perky rust and yellow mums in giant pots trimmed the street corners and proclaimed an effort to spruce things up. On one small lot between the Tress and Tan Salon and the Expresso Yourself Coffee Shop was an open area made into a concrete park. In the center perched a gazebo bracketed by two cement benches and more of the giant flowerpots filled with mums, a splash of vibrant color on a sunny day.

Whisper Falls was a town torn between the old and the new, the run-down and the revitalized. And she liked it.

With a start Annalisa realized they'd reached their destination—a pharmacy recessed into the walls of an old brick building but with modern plate glass along the front.

She lifted her face from the cool window to look at the cowboy. "I told you—"

"Give me the prescription."

"You don't have to…"

With a warning scowl, he took the paper from her fingers, slammed out of the truck and went inside a double glass door. Fancy script proclaimed Jessup's Pharmacy alongside a stenciled mortar and pestle in black silhouette. The old red brick was a beauty with 1884 engraved on the gingerbread top and a turquoise tiled entry from the sidewalk to the doors.

A pair of women about her age entered the pharmacy behind Austin. One pushed a baby stroller. An older couple passed by, the man treading patiently beside a bent, crippled woman using a walker. Once, the tiny gray woman grinned up at her man, a flash of flirtation that touched Annalisa. She watched the come and go of locals, noting the ease and simplicity of friendly folks greeting one another. A teenager opened a door for a woman. A skipping girl dropped a handful of change and when the coins flew in every direction, a family of three stopped to help. Car doors slammed and voices called out greetings. No one seemed angry or stressed or too busy to say hello.

A deep yearning pulled at the empty spaces inside her. Did places like this really exist anymore? Did anyone's family remain intact? Did a man and woman have a chance of growing old together?

She was still pondering that question when the cowboy emerged from the pharmacy and came toward her. Some bizarre emotion—relief, confusion, attraction—bubbled up. *Attraction?* Where had that come from?

Austin opened the truck door and tossed a white paper sack onto the seat. Pills inside clicked together as paper rustled.

A battle raged inside Annalisa. The need for help warred with the need to get out of the truck and stop imposing on a stranger. An attractive stranger.

"Thank you. I'll repay you as soon as I can."

"Forget it." He sat there for a full minute, staring through the windshield at the pharmacy.

Struggling with the uncomfortable notion that some twisted portion of her brain found any man attractive, Annalisa clutched the pharmacy sack like a life preserver. He'd rescued her from the woods, taken her to the doctor, bought her medication. Now what? Where did she go from here?

Chapter Three

To her credit, his sister hadn't beeped a word of surprise when Austin returned to the ranch with burgers, fries and Annalisa Keller in tow. He was glad. He was no mood to explain his annoying need to make sure Annalisa was all right, particularly because he had no explanation other than sympathy. The woman was in a fix, and even if she was liar, she was injured, alone and penniless.

He hoped he wasn't harboring a fugitive.

With the scent of fresh burgers and fried apple pies tantalizing the kitchen, the three congregated around the wooden table and fell upon the food like starving cougars.

From behind his burger, Austin watched Annalisa and pondered. She was kick-in-the-gut pretty, probably late twenties like Cassie and as anxious as he was. He wished he wasn't so intrigued.

"Still got a calf out there somewhere," he said,

more to get his mind off the mysterious woman than because he worried about the calf.

"Too dark to go after her now," Cassie said. "Maybe her mama will bawl her home."

"Hopefully." At first light, he'd be out searching. He'd be on the lookout for other things, too.

"Were you hunting for the calf this afternoon," Annalisa asked, "when you…found me instead?"

Her worried expression made Austin want to reassure her. He didn't know why. Nothing about this day made sense. "Calves get out all the time."

She hadn't said much other than a thousand thank-yous that were starting to set his teeth on edge. He didn't want thanks. He wanted her to go away so he could stop worrying about her.

But if she did, he'd worry more. What if she was in trouble? What if she was like Blair…

He put the brakes on *that* runaway train. Annalisa Keller was a stranger who would be gone as soon she finished that jumbo, everything-piled-inside burger. He didn't know where she'd go, but she was going. End of subject.

In a dainty motion that enthralled him, the woman on his mind folded the carryout paper napkin in tidy thirds and patted her mouth. The action inadvertently drew Austin's attention to the shape and curve of bowed lips and to the pale strain pulling the corners down. Her upper lip was still puffy but nothing like before. The red streaks on her throat had faded, as well. Whatever had happened was fresh when he'd found her at the waterfall.

She'd had a tough day. The protective male in him wanted to do something to make things better, but how could he when she wouldn't tell the truth? He gnawed the edge of his burger, amazed at his line of thinking. Something about this woman got to him, and that was dangerous.

Her hair, wet from the waterfall, had dried and apparently Cassie had loaned her a brush because the golden blond waves curved neatly to her shoulders. Two thick, lazy curls framed her forehead and bracketed her cheekbones and eyes. Again, he noted the strain and the beginnings of bruises on her cheek and temple.

"You look pretty rough," he said. "Exhausted, too."

"Austin!" Cassie scolded. "No girl wants to hear that."

"Well, look at her."

Annalisa's gaze moved back and forth between the brother and sister. "I am a little tired. If I could impose on you for a ride to a shelter or a hostel…"

"What are you talking about, girl?" Cassie laid aside her burger and reached out to pat Annalisa's arm. "Tomorrow is soon enough to worry about that. You've been through too much for one day.

You're staying right here tonight, isn't she, Austin?"

Austin choked on a French fry. He'd been thinking more like renting her a hotel room. "I—uh—"

"Of course she is." Cassie threw down her napkin and rose. "Annalisa, if you're finished eating, come with me, and I'll show you the guest room. Once you get some rest, everything will look much better."

As if she had no argument left in her, Annalisa took the white pharmacy bag from the table and followed Cassie.

Still sputtering, Austin watched in sheer dread as his sister ushered a total stranger down the hall and out of sight. A stereotypical hairdresser, Cassie was a people person with a real knack for listening and counseling. She probably knew more about the citizens of Whisper Falls than anyone. And if she'd decided to pry into Annalisa's personal life, she would.

Cows and horses and hay meadows Austin could control. Like women in general, his sister was out of his league.

He could hear Cassie's chatter, like a tour guide, talking about towels and extra blankets and one of his T-shirts. His brain skittered to a stop. Cassie was loaning Annalisa one of his T-shirts?

He squeezed his eyes shut and shook his head. That was not an image he wanted to entertain.

Stuffing the rest of the burger in his mouth, he got up to clean the kitchen. Cassie managed to get out of cooking and cleaning most nights. She might be a good listener, but she despised housework.

By the time Cassie returned, humming as if she'd done her good deed for the day, Austin was elbow-deep in soap suds.

"You should buy us a dishwasher," she said blithely. It was an ongoing discussion between them.

"I don't mind washing dishes. Grab a towel."

"You are so weird." She opened a drawer and pulled out a towel. "Guys don't like doing dishes."

Austin lifted a handful of suds and let them slide through his fingers. "Suds therapy. Keeps me from throttling my sister."

She sniffed and tossed her head. "You need some kind of therapy."

He flipped suds at her. "Is this your night to insult your big brother? Don't forget, I brought the burgers. You're supposed to be nice to me."

"True." Cassie swirled the towel around a red plate. "I like her."

"Who?"

She rolled her eyes. "Annalisa. She seems nice."

"She's hiding something."

Glass clattered as Cassie opened the cabinet

and slid dishes inside. "You like her, too. I saw you watching her."

"Don't even go there. I was watching her because she's a liar, and I'm a suspicious man."

Cassie ignored him, something she did on a regular basis. "I invited her to stay with us for a few days until she gets things figured out."

Austin's hands clenched around a fork. Tines poked him. "You did what?"

"You heard me. And don't act all surprised. *You're* the one who brought her here. Twice."

"I didn't know what else to do."

In a quiet tone, Cassie nailed him. "Neither does she."

Austin wrestled with his conscience. He was as sympathetic as the next person, but having Annalisa under his roof more than one day bothered him. A lot.

"Something's way off base with this woman, Cassie. Why won't she explain herself?"

"Maybe she has a good reason. Maybe she's scared. Maybe she's not sure who she can trust."

He'd wondered about that. "Did you notice that she's never asked to call anyone? She has no personal effects, nowhere to go. What if she's a criminal or worse?"

"What could be worse?"

"There's worse, and you know it." He shot her a meaningful look.

"Austin," she said gently.

"Don't want your sympathy, Cassie. I want your cooperation. For once, agree with me on something." Taking in a troubled woman was setting himself up for a fall he couldn't take. Not again. Irritation edging toward fear, Austin rinsed a plate and shoved it toward his nosy sister. "Something is way out of line, and I don't want to be involved."

He'd bought this ranch out in the middle of nowhere for a reason. He wanted peace, quiet and solitude. He'd wanted to be as far away from speculation and suspicion as humanly possible.

Adding a lying stranger with a broken arm to the mix wouldn't work.

"You can't hide from people forever, Austin. Life goes on."

He jerked the plug from the drain. Water gurgled. "Don't go there." There were some things he didn't talk about, even to Cassie. "This is my house and I said no. Tomorrow she goes."

"Where?"

"That's her business. Not yours. Not mine."

His sister slapped a hand on the counter. "She's staying. She's broke and injured—a soul in need. God sent her to us."

He scoffed in the back of his throat. "I don't believe that garbage."

"Your unbelief doesn't change the truth." Cassie stood perfectly still, an unusual phenomenon, and asked in her sweetest voice, "Come on, Austin, please. Annalisa needs a place to stay for a few days while her arm mends and she figures out… something. We have room. We can help her. It's not a big deal."

"It's the something she needs to figure out that bothers me. She should be straight up with us, tell us what's going on."

"Maybe she will when she feels more comfortable."

Her words chafed at him. He didn't like when his sister was right.

He yanked the towel from the rack to dry his hands. "I don't like it."

"You like *her*. I think that's the problem. It's been so long since you've noticed a woman—"

Austin spun, pointing a finger. "Three days tops. And then she's out of here. Got it?"

Cassie shot him a wounded look, lips tight and resentful. "As you said, it's *your* house."

She flounced out of the room as fast as her ladybug slippers could flap against hardwood. Austin watched her go, feeling both victory and defeat.

He didn't want her here.

Annalisa leaned against the crack of the bedroom door, listening to the brother and sister conversation. Austin Blackwell wanted her gone. Truth be told, she wanted the same thing.

Whirling, she went to the extension telephone on the cherry dresser and lifted the receiver. Just as quickly she put the instrument down.

Who would she call? Olivia wouldn't answer. And Annalisa had burned her bridges with Reverend Beaker. Her boss? She laughed a soft, bitter laugh. Her boss was James, the last man she'd ever call. James held the keys to her life. She'd handed him everything and received nothing but sorrow in return. As of today, she was alone, broke and unemployed.

Tormented with regret, she sagged on the side of the bed. Thank God the cowboy and his sister had taken her in. Otherwise, she'd be sleeping under a tree, cold and hurt and alone.

Her body ached all over, even her scalp where James had held her hair while he'd broken her arm.

She resisted the image. No use reliving the nightmare. He was gone. Hopefully, he'd never look back. He was like that. He'd blow hot and then cold, and if he decided she was too much trouble, he wouldn't give her a second thought. He'd find another woman by tomorrow.

The painful truth shamed her further. How had she let herself get involved with a man like James

Winchell? How could she have loved a man who showed so little care and respect for her?

Annalisa knew the answer and she didn't like it—a woman who didn't respect herself.

She pushed a hand through her hair. No use dwelling on James tonight. She roamed aimlessly around the tidy room, wondering about the owners. Friendly Cassie with the red lipstick and ebony hair who'd insisted she stay against Austin's wishes. Austin. Rugged, handsome cowboy. Gruff and aloof, he both scared and fascinated her.

Would she never learn?

A breath of frustration and fatigue stirred the air.

Nothing fancy here in the Blackwells' guest room, but homey and pleasant. Sage walls and white woodwork. A cherry sleigh bed covered in a beige-and-brown quilt and piled high with pillows. A red throw tossed over an easy chair next to the double windows.

Annalisa went to the window and gazed out. The night was deep and black. Except for the stars and moon, only the single floodlight near the barn shed any light. Quiet. Peaceful. Yet the silence made her jittery.

Cast pressed to her side, she tried wiggling her fingers as the doctor had ordered. Her arm hurt but not as bad as she'd expected. The pain pill she'd taken had started to make her sleepy.

From the kitchen she caught the rise and fall of voices. Male and female. Austin Blackwell didn't like her but he'd helped her. She didn't understand him. But then, she clearly didn't understand men in general.

Though tempted, she didn't listen in on their conversation again. Tomorrow she'd figure out what to do. One thing for certain, she could not go back to California. At least not for a while. She couldn't go home to Kansas, either. Not until she was strong enough, brave enough, healthy enough to face her regrets and start over alone.

A knot of longing filled her with an ache greater than the one in her arm.

Fresh from an awkward, one-handed bath, she lay down on the fluffy pillow, remembering her conversation at the doctor's office. Dr. Ron had said people prayed beneath the falls expecting an answer. Was that true? Did God work that way?

She thought again of the thunderous waterfall and her whispered, desperate prayer for help, for change, for some intangible she knew was missing in her life.

Had God been listening?

As she fell asleep, she prayed again, hoping with all her heart that the story was true.

The next morning, inside the warm confines of the barn and surrounded by dust motes and the welcome smell of green hay, Austin unsaddled his horse. Hoss, the shepherd, and Jet, the graying black lab, flopped in the sunshine just inside the entryway, tongues wagging. The prissy poodle was probably still curled up in her blanket on Cassie's bed.

Austin and the two real dogs, as he called them, had been up since six riding the ridge and woods, checking fence and searching for a stray calf that didn't want to be found. He'd also been searching for Annalisa's missing handbag. He'd found neither.

Blue-and-rust swallows fluttered against the rafters, chattering their squeaky song like a dozen annoyed chipmunks. A feather floated down from above. Cisco snorted and jostled to one side. Austin rubbed a soothing hand down the horse's withers and welcomed the animal warmth. Even in his jacket, he was chilled this fall morning.

He was chilled in his soul, too. Having a woman of questionable circumstance under his roof made him nervous. He'd laid awake half the night wondering about her.

The morning ride, though, had been beautiful. He'd seen deer and coyotes and turkey and a sunrise that had made him stop on the high ridge and watch as a navy blue sky gave way to pink and gold and flame.

Still, it had been a wasted three hours.

Dogs circling his legs, Austin led the horse from the barn into the corralled lot and turned him loose. The other horses lifted their muzzles, winding their friend. Cisco moseyed away to stick his regal head in the feeder and have breakfast.

Austin's belly rumbled in response. He was ready for breakfast, too, his single cup of coffee a distant memory.

He crossed the backyard and stepped on the porch. A bacon scent greeted him as he opened the door into the kitchen. He paused, confused for a second. Cassie left for work at eight and besides, she never cooked breakfast—or anything else for that matter.

Annalisa, a spatula in her good hand, stood at the cook stove frying bacon. Tootsie sat at her feet, fuzzy peach face upturned in eager anticipation. At his entrance, Annalisa glanced over one shoulder. Austin's stomach went south.

Hunger could do that to a man, he thought, annoyed that the reaction might be anything else.

"What are you doing?" She was a guest. A hurt guest. She shouldn't be cooking.

Her smile was tentative—pretty, though, in the way it lifted beneath her cheekbones and pushed up the corners of her long, mysterious eyes. She'd carefully draped her hair around the edge of her face, but he still saw the shadow of a bruise from temple to cheek. Saw it and tensed.

"I noticed the bacon on the counter and thought..." The blue eyes skittered from him to the frying pan. "I don't know. Maybe Cassie put it there."

"Cassie doesn't cook." He'd laid the meat out to thaw, expecting to fry his own breakfast.

Her gaze snapped back to his. "I figured out that much for myself. Are you hungry? This is almost done."

Austin shifted on his boots. The situation was awkward to say the least. He wasn't accustomed to seeing anyone all day and that's the way he liked it. Conversation at nine in the morning was not welcome, and he was lousy at it anyway.

More than that, Annalisa made him uncomfortable, made him fight some irrational inner desire to go out on a limb. To do something stupid.

He considered denying his hunger and going back to the barn, but his belly wouldn't let him. The smell of bacon was a siren song he never refused. Tootsie, the little beggar, agreed. He always fried an extra slice or two for her, although he'd never admit such weakness to Cassie.

"I'll make fresh coffee."

"Already did." She hitched her chin toward the pot, dark with fresh brew.

Shucking his coat and hat, Austin poured a cup and sipped. "Good coffee."

You would have thought he'd given her a ribbon at the state fair. She beamed at him over the popping bacon. "I wasn't sure…"

She didn't seem sure of anything much. Just like him, he thought wryly.

He set his cup aside to pull a carton from the fridge. Tootsie trotted over for a look.

"Eggs?"

She nodded. "How do you like yours?"

"Cooked. However you take yours is fine." He popped four pieces of bread into the toaster.

They moved around the kitchen in tandem, a surprise to Austin because he was accustomed to being alone and doing everything for himself. The poodle frittered around their feet, staying out of the way but making sure they didn't forget her.

In minutes, Annalisa set two filled plates on the table.

"Milk or juice?" she asked, sounding like a waitress. Her eagerness provoked a sympathetic response he didn't want.

"Sit down and eat." He dragged a lattice-backed chair away from the table and pointed. Annalisa sat. So did he. Tootsie plopped at their guest's feet. Not his as usual, hers. Like Cassie, the dog had already turned traitor on him.

Fork in hand, he stared at Annalisa across the round table. "You look…better."

She looked more than better. She looked good.

Too good. Other than the shadowy bruise and the arm cast. The swelling was gone from her lip and only a small dark spot remained where her lip had bled. In a set of Cassie's yellow salon scrubs, she looked like a flower in a sunny field, and her golden hair curved this way and that around her face just begging a man to touch.

"I slept pretty well all things considered."

He certainly hadn't. "How's the arm?"

"Heavy, but not hurting."

"You didn't have to do this." He waved his fork around the table. "Cook, I mean. I fend for myself."

He leaned down with a piece of bacon to lure Tootsie to his side. She trotted over, plopped on her curly bottom and took the bacon with dainty teeth. Cassie had stuck a red bow next to the dog's ear, a ridiculous thing that made Tootsie look sillier than usual.

"Breakfast was the least I could do to repay you. You and your sister… I don't know what I would have done…" She clammed up, focused on her filled plate.

Austin plowed into his breakfast, watching her, thinking. Why didn't she just come clean?

Finally, she lifted her fork and ate, too.

After a long silence, she put her toast aside and did the trifold napkin trick before dabbing her lips.

He tried not to notice those lips, shiny with bacon grease and just the right shade of pink.

"I've been thinking about my dilemma," she started.

He was thinking about the same thing. Only problem, he didn't know exactly what her dilemma was.

"I looked for your purse."

She blinked in surprise. "Oh."

"I didn't find anything. But you know that, don't you? I didn't find the bag because it's not out there."

A pink flush crested her cheeks. Her gaze dropped to her plate, but she didn't respond.

"Look, lady, I don't know you. I don't know what your problem is, but lying isn't the answer." Tempted to demand she shoot straight or hit the road, he poked a strip of bacon in his mouth. Cassie would have his head if he kicked Annalisa out today. He'd promised three days, and even though he chafed with that knowledge, he'd stick by his word. Three days and no more.

"I could have looked for a month, and I wouldn't have found your purse, would I?"

When she just sat there, eyes down and silent like a condemned prisoner, Austin got mad. Jaw tight, he raised his voice and growled, "Would I?"

She jerked and pulled her arms in tight against her body. Oversize eyes stood out against a pale face. Tootsie abandoned Austin and rose up to rub her nose against Annalisa's thigh.

Even a dog was better with women than he was.

In a whisper, Annalisa admitted. "No. I'm sorry."

Her reaction made Austin angrier. She acted like a kicked dog. She was here on his ranch, eating his breakfast. The least she could do was talk to him.

"Just spit it out. Why were you hiding under Whisper Falls? Why are you alone in a strange place without a car or money or a phone number to call?"

Annalisa sucked in her bottom lip. Her chest rose and fell and Austin had the awful feeling she might tear up. He tightened his grip on the fork. Give him a bucking horse and a kicking cow any day over a crying woman. He shouldn't have yelled. She was already scared of something.

Reining in his frustration, he lifted a hand in a plea of peace. "I had no right to yell at you. Your business is yours. You don't have to tell me anything."

But that awful nagging voice in his head said he couldn't keep her safe if he didn't know the enemy. Visions of Blair circled in his brain like vultures waiting to pick at his wounds. Enemies come in all shapes and sizes, some of them within.

A pulse of tension throbbed in the space between Austin and his houseguest. He watched a dozen emotions move over her face and didn't understand any of them.

As if she needed the contact, Annalisa absently stroked Tootsie's fuzzy head.

Austin's arms itched with the need to hold her, to send her demons fleeing. The thought shocked him to the core. He'd vowed never to get that close to a woman again. In less than a day, Annalisa had him thinking insane thoughts.

Yet, the yearning did not subside.

In a voice so low, Austin had to lean in to hear her over the hum of the fridge, she said, "I'll find another place to stay. Don't worry about me."

Too late.

"I said you could stay here for a day or two."

"But you don't want me."

Oh, yes, he did. The notion came out of nowhere, a notion so bizarre and undesirable that Austin was tempted to run out the door, mount Cisco and ride as far and fast as he could. Right behind the idea came another. Give her money. Send her away.

Yes, that's exactly what he'd do.

"There are a few bed-and-breakfast places in town. I'll give you the money. You can pay me later."

"I couldn't."

"Do you have a choice?"

Blue eyes flashed up to meet his. He saw defi-nce and defeat in the same glance. "Not at the moment."

"All right, then. It's settled." He leaned back, almost sighing with relief. After breakfast she would be out of his life, out of his house. Gone.

Cassie would have a fit.

Annalisa rose and began gathering up the dirty dishes. The poodle followed her.

"Leave those."

"I want to do them."

She went to the sink and he followed, noticing then what he hadn't before. She'd been up a while and she'd been busy. The vacuum cleaner sat next to the broom on one wall. How she'd managed to use either with one arm befuddled him, but she had. The clothes drier buzzed from the utility room, and he realized she'd done laundry, too. That explained the yellow scrubs.

As he put away the butter and jelly, she ran water to wash the dishes. One thing he'd say for her, she might wear sissy shoes, but she wasn't lazy. Even with one hand, she was willing to earn her keep.

He bumped her out of the way. Dishes with one hand would take too long. He had work to do. "I wash. You dry."

She didn't argue but took up a dish towel and waited, leaning her cast on the counter—a splash of lime green against black-and-brown granite.

"Do you know any place in town I might find a job?"

Austin frowned. "You're planning to stay in Whisper Falls?"

"Maybe. It seems to be a nice, quiet town."

"You have family here?"

She pressed her lips, looked away, moody. "No. No family."

Odd, he thought, to relocate with no family, no job, no personal belongings. "I can ask around."

"Thank you."

He held out a cup and when she reached to take it, he didn't let go. Her gaze fluttered up, startled, and he saw panic rising.

"What are you afraid of, Annalisa? No one here will hurt you." He knew as sure as he knew her eyes were the purest blue he'd ever seen, someone *had* hurt her. "Who did this? Who hurts you? Your husband? Is that it? Are you running from your husband?"

The last part stuck in his craw, a wad thick enough to choke him.

She stared at him across the cup that joined their hands. A tiny muscle twitched beneath her cheekbone. Finally, she licked her lips and whispered, "Boyfriend."

Austin released the cup along with the breath he hadn't known he was holding. He vacillated between relief that she wasn't tangled up with an abusive husband and fury at her jerk of a boyfriend.

"He broke your arm and dumped you out at the waterfall?"

"I ran. He pushed me out of the car and tried to…" She bit down on her lip, eyes wide with the painful memory. "I ran into the woods, praying he wouldn't follow me."

"Did he?"

"I don't think so. I think he'll go back to San Diego without me."

"San Diego?" That explained a few things. His mystery lady was a long way from home.

"We were on our way to a conference in Nashville. James likes to drive, to make a vacation out of business trips." Her lips twisted. "To rip off the big bosses anytime he can, although he has all of them fooled. I saw the sign about the waterfall and wanted to see it."

"What happened?"

She lifted one shoulder as if the load she carried was too heavy. "James doesn't need much to lose his temper. Hopefully, he went on to the conference."

"But you aren't sure? He could still be around, maybe in town waiting for you to show up again?"

"Possibly." Her lip trembled.

Great. Just terrific. "Was this the first time he hurt you?"

"No." Her face darkened with a fierce determination. "But it's the last. I won't go back. I won't see him again. No matter what he does."

Rage boiled in Austin's gut. If he could get his hands on that jerk… "Maybe you should call the cops."

Not that he wanted anything to do with cops.

Hands raised in a defensive gesture, she jerked back in panic. "No! Please. I can't. Don't say anything. I'll leave here today and won't bother you again. Only promise you won't tell anyone, especially the police."

"A scum like that shouldn't get away with hurting a woman."

"The police won't help. Trust me. I've tried."

In a way, he understood her reluctance. The police weren't always helpful. Sometimes they were dead wrong.

Austin gazed into her pretty face and saw fear. He heard the tremor in her voice and the desperation.

A heaviness came down around him, a cloak of responsibility and dread. He knew what he was about to do and he didn't like it one bit.

No matter how much he wanted Annalisa Keller to leave, he couldn't send her away.

For the next few days or weeks or months, until his conscience would let her go, Annalisa was here to stay.

Chapter Four

Annalisa braced the broom beneath her cast and swept the porch with her good arm. Tootsie, the funny little poodle, darted back and forth, growling and nipping at the broom straw.

Three days had passed. Three days that would have been pleasant if not for the ax hanging over her head. Her time at the Blackwell ranch was up and she had nowhere to go.

Each morning, Cassie went off to work at the Tress and Tan Salon and didn't return until dinnertime, usually with a pizza or other fast food. Last night, after a meal of takeout tacos, she'd painted Annalisa's toenails. Annalisa glanced down at her bare feet, smiling a little at the orange-and-black tiger stripes. She'd forgotten how much fun a friend, or a sister, could be. She and Olivia had done that kind of thing. A long time ago.

With a sad ache beneath her rib cage, she paused

to look out over the peaceful yard, thinking about the strangeness of life. She missed Olivia with a depth as raw as her emotions. How had she let anything or anyone come between her and her only blood kin?

She had a plethora of questions, most of them for herself. How had she ever come to be here, in this place, at this moment? If she hadn't asked to see the waterfalls, James wouldn't have gotten angry, and she would have gone right on to Tennessee and then back to California. Maybe. Or maybe he would have become angry about something else. Sooner or later, he always did.

Yet in some twisted way or for some twisted reason, she'd thought herself in love with him. What was wrong with her? Where had her life gotten off course?

"God, I am so broken," she whispered to the wispy clouds. "How can I ever put myself back together when half the pieces are missing?"

The sky didn't answer and the gnawing emptiness in her chest spread. Fear and yearning had been her companions for such a long time that they'd supplanted more positive emotions. She'd become a black hole, devoid of joy.

Yet, two strangers had thrown out a life preserver. Reluctant though he may have been, Austin Blackwell and his sister had done more for her in three days than the man to whom she'd given her love and her life.

But her time was up. Somehow she had to find a way to make it on her own without help, without James.

At the memory of her ex-boyfriend, dread, like an iron weight, pressed down on her shoulders. Tension tightened the muscles of her neck.

She glanced to the right and then the left, irrationally afraid that James would come crashing through the brush and find her.

A slight breeze ruffled the leaves of a nearby chinquapin oak, bringing with it the scent of moist, fertile earth and gathering autumn. Peace and quiet reigned here in the remote Ozarks, but she struggled to relax for more than a moment at a time.

If she was jumpy here, how would she feel once she left this ranch and the people who'd given her a modicum of safety?

Acorns thudded to the ground and a pair of squirrels raced down the shingled bark after the feast.

Tootsie gave them little more than a glance.

By sheer force of will, she focused on the poodle and closed the mental door on James.

"Lazy," she murmured, gently touching the dog's paw with her toe. Tootsie rewarded her with a doggy smile and bright button eyes. "Nothing like your master."

Each morning after a shared breakfast, Austin made himself scarce. She wondered if he always worked without stopping, or if he was avoiding contact with her. She felt guilty to think she might be keeping him from his usual routine. This was, after all, his home, his solitude, which he apparently preferred to her company.

Who could blame him for that? She was the interloper. No doubt, Austin Blackwell considered her a pathetic excuse for a woman and couldn't wait to get her out of his house. She'd talked to him about James which was probably a mistake. She still didn't know why she'd opened up, considering she'd never told anyone.

"Desperate measures," she murmured and earned a cocked ear from the comical dog. She'd needed the Blackwells. She needed them still, but the fact remained, Austin had given her three days.

To repay their kindness, she'd cleaned and cooked and done laundry. None of that was enough, of course. She had to move on. Even though Austin hadn't mentioned the three-day limit again, self-preservation dictated finding a job before he showed her the door.

Rubbing at the itchy juncture of cast and upper

arm, she wondered who would hire a one-armed employee with no references or identification?

If she wasn't such a coward she'd call James and demand he send her belongings.

Not that he'd ever responded to any of her demands. The more she wanted something, the more stubbornly James held back.

She wondered where he was now and what he was doing. Would he look for her? What would he say to their friends and colleagues when she didn't return? She'd put him in a difficult situation and she knew very well he wouldn't take her betrayal lightly. That's the way James thought. This was her fault. Sometimes she wondered if he was right.

With a soul-heavy sigh, she looked out at the quiet acreage flowing away from Blackwell Ranch in shades of green and gold. Black cows dotted green fields. A pair of calves bucked and played, tails twitching over their backs. Miles of fence disappeared into the woods that led to Whisper Falls, the falls where she'd hidden from James and prayed.

She thought about that prayer, had thought about it a lot. Just as she pondered the man who claimed to love her and the cowboy who'd rescued her that day.

Tootsie suddenly yipped and spun to face the tree-covered mountain, floppy ears lifting out to each side. Annalisa reached behind her to the door handle, ready to escape inside. She'd heard nothing from James, but she was not brave enough to believe he would let her go without retribution.

The two big dogs, Hoss and Jet, broke through the distant woods and raced across the pasture pink tongues flapping, toward the quivering, prancing Tootsie.

Some of her tension drained away.

When Austin and his horse appeared directly behind the dogs, Annalisa's scalp prickled. Her grip tightened on the door knob. Too much thinking about James had made her unduly jittery. She had no reason to fear the cowboy. He might be abrupt but he'd also been kind. So far.

Loose and easy in the saddle, Austin rode the horse directly to the edge of the porch, bringing with him the smells of deep woods and heated horseflesh. Annalisa propped the broom in the crook of her cast to stroke Cisco's velvety nose.

"You all right?" Austin leaned forward in the saddle, leather shifting as he patted the horse's neck.

A funny little hitch caught in Annalisa's throat. That was always the first thing he asked and somehow, the thoughtful question made her feel something she hadn't experienced in a long time. She felt cared about and protected—by a man she barely knew. "Except for this awful itching on my arm, I'm fine. Are you hungry?"

Offering to feed him was her defense against the rush of emotions welling up inside her. For the past three days she'd wondered if she was having some kind of nervous breakdown. At the smallest kindness, tears came unbidden. Yet, she felt pathetically starved for kind words.

"Thanks, but I'm good." Stirrups groaned as he grasped the saddle horn with one gloved hand and swung easily to the ground. "I'll grab something in town."

The pair of big dogs flopped onto the porch with a groan. Tootsie danced around their noses only to be sniffed once or twice and then ignored.

"You're going into town?" Stupid question. He'd just said as much.

"In a bit." He removed his hat and gloves and tossed them onto a wooden Adirondack chair next to the back door. His black hair curled around his ears and stuck up in one spot where his hat had pulled. Annalisa found that one stray curl immeasurably and uncomfortably appealing.

"Shouldn't you tie the horse?"

"He won't go anywhere." But he turned back long enough to drop the reins to the grass. "See? Ground tied."

"Good horse."

"You know the old saying. A cowboy is entitled

to one good horse, one good dog and one good woman. Cisco's my one good horse."

She didn't recognize the adage, but for the sake of conversation, Annalisa glanced at the pair of dogs spread like rugs next to the door. "If you can only choose one…"

Austin grinned and shook his head. "Don't ask."

Annalisa marveled at the change in Austin when he smiled. The simple act of upturned lips, of a softened face wielded such power. Attractive power.

By this time, Tootsie had given up on playing with Hoss and Jet to dance a circle around Austin on her hind legs. He scooped her up and rubbed her ears. "It's sure not you, old girl. You're not even a real dog."

"I won't tell Cassie you said that." Annalisa opened the back door and stepped inside the kitchen, acutely aware of the handsome cowboy at her back. Her pulse fluttered, but this time the reason had nothing to do with fear. His comment about "one good woman" rattled around in her head. Was there a woman in Austin's life?

"Cassie and Darrell wanted kids, but when that didn't work out, she bought this dog." Austin stooped to release the poodle, looking chagrinned. "Sorry. My mouth runs away sometimes."

Annalisa almost laughed. The man was as tight-lipped with personal conversation as an undercover cop. "Cassie told me."

"She did?" He scratched at one ear. "Darrell's accident hit her hard. She doesn't usually talk about it."

From Cassie, she'd learned about her new husband's death in a boating accident. She'd also learned that Cassie didn't discuss the tragedy with Austin because she thought her grief upset her brother. "Understandable, don't you think? They'd been married what? Four days?"

"Yeah." Shoulders tense, Austin went to the refrigerator and took out a container of juice.

Annalisa could tell he was every bit as uncomfortable discussing Darrell with her as with Cassie. She changed the subject.

Even though worried he'd refuse, she had to ask, "Would you mind a hitchhiker when you go into town?"

He poured a tall glass of OJ. "You sure it's safe for you to be seen in public?"

"I can't hide in your house forever, Austin. Nor can I continue to impose on your hospitality indefinitely."

He scowled and those black eyebrows came together in a forbidding vee. "You're not imposing."

"My three-day limit is up today."

The scowl deepened. "Did Cassie tell you that?"

"No, you told me."

He rocked back on his bootheels. "Me? I never said any such thing. I said…"

She let him off the hook. "Look, Austin, I know you didn't want me to stay here. I understand." Sort of. "That's why it's imperative I either find a job in Whisper Falls or…"

"Or what, Annalisa?" His voice was soft, and the ever-ready tears pushed up behind her eyes again. Even though Austin didn't know it, he'd tapped into one of her deepest worries. Her choices were few. She had nowhere else to go, no one to turn to other than to a man who abused her, and no accessible money.

She'd called her bank in California, only to discover she could not retrieve her account without the number—a number found on her checks and bank cards, all of which were in James's possession.

"I have money in the bank. I just can't get it out without going back to my apartment or calling James." Her stomach churned to think of having a conversation with James at this juncture.

"James." Austin's lips parted, teeth bared like a wolf warning off a predator. "The boyfriend?"

"Yes, James. He has my purse, remember?" All her other belongings, too, but she wasn't ready to share every detail of her misspent life with a man on whose charity she depended. *Charity.* The word stuck in her throat like a swallowed bug.

"That's why I have to find work. I can't even buy another set of clothes, and I can't keep borrowing from Cassie."

"We'll figure out something."

"It's not your problem."

"You made it my problem when you whacked me with that rock." He tossed back the juice glass for a long swallow. His throat, strong and sun-browned above the open neck of his button-up, flexed as he drained the glass.

Attraction fluttered, an unwelcome moth in her belly. Annalisa forced her attention away from the masculine sight. "I'm sorry."

"You should be."

Annalisa's gaze flew back to his. Was he angry? Would he— The thoughts skittered to a halt. She drew in a deep breath to calm her jittery nerves. Austin Blackwell was nothing like James.

Austin gave her a long, appraising look before saying, "I'm leaving in thirty minutes. Be ready."

At Cassie's request, Austin dropped Annalisa at the beauty salon first. Then he'd stopped at the feed store before heading over to the Iron Horse Snack Shop. He strode inside, drawn by the smell of owner Evelyn Parsons's homemade apple pie and the need to ask a few questions. If anyone in town knew where a woman with a broken arm could find work, Evelyn or her husband, Digger, would know.

Austin suffered a twinge of guilt over his eagerness to be rid of his troubling visitor. The guilt was followed quickly by the more confounding worry that nagged him like a toothache. James the jerk was out there somewhere and by now he could be heading back this way from Tennessee. The question remained: If Annalisa's boyfriend showed his face in Whisper Falls, what then? Would Austin's conscience, the squealing troublemaker, allow him to throw Annalisa to the wolves?

Probably not.

She'd been nervous when he'd ridden in on Cisco this morning. He'd spotted the white-knuckled hand on the doorknob and the way she'd stood, hyper-alert.

The man he had once been wanted to protect her. The coward he'd become wanted her gone.

"Austin, how are you doin', boy?" a chipper voice called. "Hadn't seen you in a coon's age."

Uncle Digger Parsons manned the snack bar today, a white dish towel slung over one ample shoulder. As far as Austin could ascertain, Uncle Digger was no one's uncle but everyone called him that. The sixtysomething man ran the town's tourist train, a daily three-hour excursion through the Ozark Mountains that had grown in popularity since the Whisper Falls marketing ploy. People came from miles around to board the train and spend their money while Uncle Digger spouted railroad sayings with the same gusto as the bright red engine spouted smoke.

Uncle Digger, along with Evelyn, or Miss Evelyn as she was known to the locals, also kept the depot museum in shape and knew practically everything about the town's history. When his wife wasn't around, Uncle Digger served up coffee and premade sandwiches, fruit and snacks, and of course, Miss Evelyn's almost-famous homemade pie along with a hearty dose of country wisdom.

Even though Austin steered clear of too much community involvement, he got a kick out of visiting with Uncle Digger. In striped overalls and a gold-braided conductor's cap, the portly gent was a little wise, a little crazy and moved with the speed of a turtle. To him, the world of railroad dominance had never ended so he lived and breathed railroad history.

"Been busy." Austin threw a leg over a bar stool and removed his hat.

"So's I heard."

"That right?"

"Cassie was in earlier. Her and Evelyn's got themselves a full head of steam over the beautifying committee." He said all this without moving a muscle other than the furry mustache draped around his mouth like a squirrel's tail.

"The town looks good." Not that Austin paid much attention to flowerpots and such.

"Sure enough does. Right on track for Pumpkin Fest. I'm telling you, son, internet marketing is a pure marvel. A few years back no one had ever heard of Whisper Falls, and now the motels are filled up all summer. Then come December, folks show up again for an old-fashioned mountain Christmas. Yes, sir, prayer is a powerful thing."

Austin's lips twitched, although whether in amusement or cynicism, he couldn't say. "Prayer or marketing?"

Uncle Digger chuckled. "Well, now, son, the Lord expects us to use whatever He gives us. It just took us a while to figure out how to do that."

"The story about praying under the waterfall was your idea, right?"

"Well, mine and Evelyn's. And the good Lord's, of course. Pudge Loggins started the whole thing. Me and Evelyn, we just stoked the coals."

"What did Pudge have to do with it?" Austin had purchased fishing lures from Pudge Loggins's bait and tackle shop. He was an affable guy, round as a barrel, with enormous black plastic glasses and a habit of laughing at the end of every sentence.

"Well, now, here's the deal." Uncle Digger stroked

his mustache and settled his elbow on the counter, eager to spin the tale. "Old Pudge, he'd all but given up on getting a bank loan to open his store. The banker said the economy was bad. He claimed that Whisper Falls, which was plain old Millerville back then, needed a fishing store like a Rockerfeller needs another penny. Poor old Pudge, his caboose was dragging, let me tell you."

The wooden door creaked open and a customer entered the Iron Horse.

"Mayor," Digger said and nodded once but stayed put at the counter.

"Uncle Digger." The boyish mayor took a doughnut from a glass display case, poured himself a cup of coffee and settled at a table where the weekly newspaper was already spread open.

Paying the customer no further attention, Uncle Digger went on with the tale.

"One day Pudge was out roaming the woods, feeling sorry for himself when all of a sudden he got the notion to climb down behind the falls. Folks say he was going to jump in but that's not the way Pudge tells it."

"You think he would have?" Had Annalisa considered the same thing? Was that her reason for climbing down the ledge? Was she that depressed? The notion filled him with a new worry. Depression was an evil malady.

"Nah, not Pudge. He's too scared of Ruby

Faye to drown himself." Uncle Digger paused to chuckle at his own joke. "Anyhoo, he says he never understood why, but just like that, the biggest urge came over him to pray."

Austin controlled the need to roll his eyes. He'd had the same urges once upon a time. Fat lot of good they'd done him.

"So he did," Uncle Digger went on. "He told the Big Conductor in the Sky about how he wanted that little store and all. And wouldn't you know it? By the time he got back to town, still dripping wet and lower than a train tunnel, the banker was calling him on the phone."

"To approve the loan?"

Uncle Digger nodded. "Sure enough. And afterward, Pudge told everybody about praying under the waterfall right before the call. Pretty soon there was a trail of folks headed that way in search of a miracle. Before we knew it, prayers were getting answered all over the place."

In spite of a strong dose of skepticism, Austin asked, "What kind of prayers?"

Uncle Digger rubbed his craggy jaw. "Well, let's see. Mary and Dale Craddock's marriage was derailed, gone plumb off the track and ready to call it quits. Then Mary went up there to pray and next thing you know, they're off to Hawaii on a second honeymoon."

"Could have been a coincidence."

Uncle Digger arched an eyebrow. "Coincidence? Why, Austin, don't you know a coincidence is just a case of God remaining anonymous?"

"Hadn't heard that one." Didn't believe it, either.

"Yes, sir. The Lord's working on our behalf all the time. If we ain't asleep at the wheel, we'll notice. And that, my boy, is how me and Evelyn came up with the idea."

The marketing strategy was harmless, Austin supposed, but it seemed less than honest to him.

"Everyone needs the Lord's help. Sometimes they just don't know how to find it. So we figured to do our part in steering folks in the right direction. The Good Book says that God's people perish for a lack of knowledge. By putting the testimonies of answered prayers out on the internet, folks can learn and get their needs met. Why, it's a beautiful thing."

The cynic in Austin had to say, "In other words, you lure people to Whisper Falls with tales of answered prayers, all the while hoping they'll stay for a burger or a ride on the train."

Uncle Digger stroked his mustache. "I see you're a doubter. Used to be one myself 'til God and that pretty little woman of mine got hold of me. Just you remember, if the Big Conductor is driving the train, everything's going to work out for the best."

If ever Austin doubted anything, he doubted that. He'd been down a road where nothing worked out, where evil prevailed and no amount of prayer or begging God made a bit of difference.

Uncle Digger gestured toward the pie case. "I guess you're wanting some of Evelyn's pie."

Relieved to move past the uncomfortable subject of prayer, Austin nodded. "Milk, too, if you have it."

"I surely do. Anything in a package or a can, I probably got it." With the pace of a snail, Uncle Digger slid a presliced pie from the pie case. Three slices were already gone and the perfectly browned crust oozed cinnamon-scented apples. "Too bad that sister of yours can't cook."

"She can. A little. But she won't."

"Never find a man that way."

"She's not looking."

"Sure she is. She just don't know it. You are, too. A man without a good woman is only going through the motions."

Austin pointed a finger. "Now wait a minute, Uncle Digger."

Uncle Digger waved a spatula at him. "Simmer down, son. I didn't mean no harm. Tell me all about her."

"Cassie?"

Uncle Digger snorted. "That pretty gal you found under Whisper Falls. Exciting tale, right there. Reckon she'll give us a testimony for the website?"

News traveled fast in small towns, but Austin had no intention of sharing Annalisa's problems with anyone. He sure didn't want anybody knowing about his.

"Not much to tell. Her name's Annalisa Keller. She's alone and looking for work. That's what I wanted to talk to you about."

"Work, you say? Well, let me think." Uncle Digger paused with spatula hiked in the air like a fly swatter while Austin's mouth watered at the sight of that crusty pie, so close and yet still several minutes away. There was no use rushing Uncle Digger. Only Miss Evelyn could do that.

The door opened again and an unfamiliar family of four came inside. A man in khaki shorts asked, "When is the next train ride?"

"Tomorrow morning, ten-thirty sharp. Just like always." Uncle Digger motioned the spatula toward the cash register. "You want to buy tickets today? You get a little discount for buying in advance."

"Might as well."

Austin's hopes for pie dwindled as Uncle Digger left the pie case in favor of a ticket sale. He considered retrieving the slice for himself, and then he thought about going down to the drive-in restaurant instead. Before he could make up his mind, other customers filtered in and behind them came the energetic, rosy-cheeked Miss Evelyn. In a whirlwind of activity, she bustled into the snack shop. That was Miss Evelyn's way. Where Uncle Digger moved as slow as a sloth, Miss Evelyn fidgeted and hurried, buzzing around like a bee after honey.

She breezed behind the counter, pecked a grinning Uncle Digger on the cheek, and asked, "Is he getting you some pie, Austin?"

"I keep hoping."

Evelyn cackled at his attempted humor and headed for the pie case to scoop out the slice he'd been dreaming about. "Milk, too?"

"Yes, ma'am. Thank you."

"I was getting it," Uncle Digger hollered, although he appeared rooted in one spot next to the ticket window.

"Never you mind, honey. We don't want the boy to starve to death. You go right on with what you're doing." She gave Austin a conspiratorial wink.

"Thanks, Miss Evelyn. Uncle Digger tells me you and Cassie are hard at work cleaning up Whisper Falls."

"We're doing our best. Your sister is a bundle of energy, and she has a thumb almost as green as mine." Evelyn slid the pie and milk in front of him along with a fork and napkin before moving on to the next customer. She could have a roomful of people served before Uncle Digger got his hands out of his pockets.

"I met your pretty visitor," she went on. "Annalisa. Isn't that the prettiest name, Digger?" The old man bobbed his head but didn't get a chance to speak. "Poor little thing with that broken arm. She's in a bad fix, that's for sure. Bless her heart."

Austin cut a bite of pie with the side of his fork and listened while Miss Evelyn dispensed soft drinks from the fountain for a local man and his two children. "Here you go, hon. Orange for Paige and grape for Nathan."

Austin had seen the trio before but couldn't place them. The man was lean and lanky and probably about Austin's age. The kids were cute, neat and clean in jeans and Ts. The little girl's hand-over-mouth giggle made Austin smile.

When the boy wrapped his arms around his daddy's neck and gushed, "You're the best dad ever," Austin got a catch in his throat. Like Cassie, Austin had wanted children and like her, life had knocked his hat in the dirt. There was still hope for Cassie to find someone and start fresh. As for himself, he wouldn't go there again. Not after Blair.

Suddenly, Uncle Digger was back, leaning across the counter. "How's the pie?"

"The best."

"Does that houseguest of yours know her way around a kitchen?"

They were back to Annalisa again. Austin shoved the last bite of sweet tender apple into his mouth, chewed and swallowed. "Better than Cassie. Why? Could you use her here in the snack shop?"

"Possibly, but she'll have to talk to the head engineer about that." Uncle Digger nudged his chin toward his wife. "She makes all the smart decisions. I just drive the train."

Evelyn swatted a dish towel at him. "Silly goose," she said with affection, her apple cheeks rosy, "I already told Annalisa to stop in after Cassie does her hair. We'll put our heads together and see what we can come up with."

Austin finished his milk and pulled out his wallet. "You don't even know her. Why put yourself out?"

"You didn't know her, either, but you stepped right up to the plate." She took his money and punched keys on the old-fashioned cash register. The drawer popped out with a *ca-ching*. "She's a good person. You can tell by the eyes. They're the windows to the soul, you know. Annalisa has good eyes. Kind of sad but pure-hearted. Real pretty girl, too, don't you think?"

Austin wasn't going to answer that.

"Did she tell you how she broke her arm?" He considered warning the older couple about the abusive boyfriend but figured that was Annalisa's place.

"Cassie said something about a fall. Bless her heart. These rocks and hills can be treacherous. Good thing we have Creed Carter and his helicopter. Why, only last week he flew Mildred Laird to Hot Springs for hip surgery."

Austin didn't bother to mention that other than the pilot's usefulness, an octogenarian falling in the bathtub was not the least connected to treacherous rocks. As far as he was concerned, Creed Carter and his chopper could fly to Mars and never come back.

"I wish he'd stick to medi-flights," he mumbled.

"Why, Austin Blackwell, tourists love the helicopter rides. That boy had a brilliant idea to fly folks over Whisper Falls and around the Ozarks."

Personally, Austin hated the noise, swooping down over his cows and pasture land all hours of the day and night.

"To hear him tell it," Uncle Digger said, "Creed Carter is living a dream. Just like us here at the depot, his business gets better all the time."

Figured. Before long, the town would be as

crowded as Las Vegas with billboards and lights flashing and traffic backed up to the state line. He shuddered at the thought. "Thanks for the pie, Miss Evelyn."

"Still the best you ever tasted?"

He jammed his hat down on his head. "Yes, ma'am. Better than my grandma's."

She beamed. "I can't for the life of me see how you stay single. A handsome cowboy like you with such a silver tongue. Lands a-mercy. Have you met Fawna Jefferson?"

"Evelyn, quit your matchmaking," Uncle Digger said from his spot next to the two children. "Fawna ain't Austin's type. She's scared silly of animals. The gal nearly derailed when little Jamie Bagley brought a turtle to her fourth-grade classroom. She'd faint smooth away at the sight of a cow or horse."

Austin's thoughts slid to Annalisa stroking Cisco's nose and the three dogs vying for her attention. She might be afraid of her boyfriend and maybe even of him, but she and animals got along fine.

Not that he cared one way or the other about Annalisa and his animals. Fact of the matter, he didn't know why he was thinking about his houseguest in the first place. The woman was taking up too much room inside his head.

"You two take it easy," he said and pushed

away from the counter, eager to leave. Just as he reached the door, it swung open.

And Annalisa walked in.

Chapter Five

Annalisa stopped in the doorway of the dimly lit train station. The building was late 1800s like many in Whisper Falls, and the walls were dotted with memorabilia from the past, mostly railroad artifacts. Overhead a pair of lazy ceiling fans stirred the smell of slightly musty wood and pine floor cleaner. On one wall, two ancient green train lanterns bracketed a railroad crossing sign.

As her eyes adjusted to the light, she spotted a man and two children sipping sodas at the counter and Austin Blackwell watching her from a bar stool. Coming at her like a torpedo was the energetic Evelyn Parsons whom she'd met at the Tan and Tress Salon less than an hour ago.

"Digger, look here," Evelyn said, smiling with hands outstretched toward Annalisa. "Isn't she the prettiest thing? Look at that hairdo. Why, if I had hair that blond, I'd go to Hollywood."

Annalisa couldn't hold back a smile. The older woman, whose salt-and-pepper curls were cropped close to her head in a tight perm, exuded energy and goodwill. Annalisa extended one hand which Evelyn clasped warmly with both of hers.

As she'd walked the two blocks from Cassie's workplace to the train depot, Annalisa had vacillated between hope for a job and the urge to catch the first flight out. Yet, something about the pretty old town and the friendly people drew her like a basket of new puppies. If nothing else, she needed some downtime in a quiet environment to think about her future as well as her past. Starting over, alone and broke, was hard.

Austin Blackwell pushed off the counter and sauntered in her direction. Expression serious, he said nothing. He had the most uncanny ability to make her feel safe and jumpy at the same time. She turned her focus on Evelyn.

"Is this a good time to talk?" she asked, anxious now that she was here, although Cassie had encouraged her to come, insisting Miss Evelyn and Uncle Digger were for real.

On the walk through town, she'd passed the pharmacy where Austin had purchased her prescription. She still marveled at the gruff kindness and even more at his refusal to discuss repayment. Austin Blackwell was a bewildering contradiction.

"Anytime is a good time for a new friend. You

come right on in here and get yourself acquainted. That handsome cuss manning the register is my man, Digger. Everyone calls him Uncle Digger. Suits him, don't you think?" Before Annalisa could say a word, Evelyn hooked her arm and propelled her forward. "You know Austin already." Austin, standing by the exit, bobbed his head, an amused quirk on his lips as the two women sailed past. "That fella with his head buried in the news is Mayor Fairchild. He'll come up for air after a few more cups of coffee and a half dozen doughnuts. These folks at the bar are locals. Davis Turner, meet Annalisa Keller. She's new in town."

Davis Turner turned his sandy brown, all-American good looks in her direction, his smile wide and infectious. "A pleasure, Annalisa. Welcome to Whisper Falls. These little urchins are my kids, Nathan and Paige."

"I'm nine," Paige announced. "Nathan's only eight. I'm older than him."

Their father's hundred-watt smile brightened. "And she never lets him forget it, either."

Annalisa's tense shoulders began to relax as she returned the smile. The kids were adorable, and the father wasn't bad, either. "It's good to meet you. All of you."

"Nice cast you've got there." Davis motioned to her arm. "I hope it's nothing serious."

From the corner of her eye, she saw Austin turn back from the door.

"Just a broken bone. I'll be good as new in no time," she quoted Dr. Ron.

"What happened? Did you get a boo-boo?" The little girl, Paige, hopped off her stool to get a closer look. She was kitten-cute with short brown hair, a thin, elfin face and a splash of russet freckles across her nose. With brown eyes as big as half dollars, the pixie haircut was perfect on her.

"I did. A pretty big boo-boo." But this was nothing. The past few years of her life had been a major boo-boo.

"Want me to pray for you?" Paige already had her hand on the green cast and her eyes closed.

Taken aback, Annalisa didn't know what to say, so she stood like a statue while the child's lips moved and her face glowed with radiance. In seconds, Paige's eyes popped open and she said, "You'll be all better now."

"Uh…thank you." That was different.

"You want to come and sit with us? Daddy will buy you a root beer, won't you, Daddy?"

Her father laughed, but Annalisa could see his daughter had embarrassed him.

"Paige," he said, "leave the lady alone."

"I'm not bothering her." She turned to Annalisa. "Am I bothering you?"

Before Annalisa could answer, Austin's voice

came from somewhere over her shoulder. "I don't think we've met. I'm Austin Blackwell."

He walked up beside her and offered a hand to Davis. "Annalisa's staying at my place."

Annalisa flushed. "Temporarily."

Miss Evelyn, who, surprisingly, had ceased talking and moving during the exchange, started up again. "Austin, why don't you have some more pie and get acquainted with Davis and these little cuties while I show Annalisa around? And don't run off. I want to talk to you about something important." She took Annalisa's elbow and guided her to the counter. "Digger, honey, get Austin some more pie."

The older gentleman touched the brim of his conductor's cap. "Coming right up. How about you, Davis? You and the kiddies want the last couple pieces? No use in good pie going to waste."

"I want some." The boy, Nathan, looked at his dad with comical hope. Smaller and fairer than his sister without the benefit of freckles, the boy would someday be the image of his handsome father.

"With ice cream on top. Okay, Daddy?" The freckled-nosed girl bounced back to her seat with all the confidence of a well-loved child. "Remember what you told the teacher? We're great kids. We deserve it."

Davis ruffled her hair. "I think maybe you do."

Annalisa wondered how different her life might have been if she and Olivia had had a father like Davis Turner.

But they hadn't and she'd already spent enough years mourning what she'd never had.

Leaving the men and children, Annalisa followed Evelyn to a tiny office with double doors, one leading in from the snack shop and the other leading out to the museum. The office wasn't much—a telephone, a computer, a small desk and a display rack of tourist information. An assortment of brightly colored brochures proclaimed antiques shops, bed-and-breakfast inns, helicopter flights over the waterfall, a romantic boat ride down Blackberry River and a prayer chapel proclaiming the most beautiful place for weddings in the state. Whisper Falls was a lovely mix of modern tourism and down-home charm.

"Sit right over there, hon." Evelyn pointed at the single chair against one wall. "And tell me all about yourself."

The hopeful haze evaporated faster than sweat under AC. She wasn't prepared to talk about herself. No way would she tell this sweet woman about James or the reasons she'd ended up in Whisper Falls.

But she had to say something.

She fidgeted, cleared her throat. It seemed stuck full of the lies she didn't want to tell. "I— There's not much to say. I'm a good worker. Honest." Most of the time. "I learn fast." *Though I didn't learn my lesson about James nearly fast enough.*

"Cassie tells me you've been down on your luck a bit."

"That's right." *Please don't ask me why.* "That's the reason I need to find employment. The Blackwells have been very kind, but I prefer to pay my own way."

"You been friends with Austin and Cassie a long time?"

"Not long."

"They're good kids." Miss Evelyn chuckled. "Well, they're kids to me. That Cassie, she's a dilly. Austin's on the quiet side. Keeps to himself, but I'm thinking he needs to come out of his shell. Maybe you can help me with that. I can't quite figure him out."

"Welcome to the club."

"You, too, huh?"

When Annalisa nodded, Miss Evelyn went on, "Got our work cut out, then. But I got me some ideas percolating."

Annalisa had no clue what she meant. "Ideas about a job?"

"About Austin."

"Oh."

"Let's talk about your employment problem first. I'll work on Austin later. Here's what I think.

Uncle Digger, bless his heart, prefers tinkering with the museum and the train to working in that snack shop. He's the perfect person to man the museum desk and tell folks all about the town and our wonderful recreational amenities. *I'm* busy as a beaver at a wood chopping contest with the city council and the tourism board, especially now when we're gearing up for Pumpkin Fest." She glanced at a giant pocket watch hanging on the wall. "I should be over at city hall right now. So what do you say? Do you want to try your hand—" she chuckled at the reference to Annalisa's broken arm "—at the snack shop? Doesn't pay much, but the work is easy, the people are friendly and you can get acquainted with practically everyone in town."

"Will you mind that I'm slow at first until I get a smaller cast?" Annalisa elevated the prohibitive green plaster, her arm frozen at a right angle.

Miss Evelyn laughed heartily. "Hon, anyone is faster than Uncle Digger. You'll do fine."

Relief flowed through Annalisa. Somehow they'd gotten past all the usual employment questions and personal history. Maybe God was watching out for her after all.

Austin stirred his fork in the puddle of melting ice cream and waited for the women to return. He didn't know what Miss Evelyn wanted with him, but she'd said it was important, and he didn't mind the wait. He worried about leaving Annalisa alone in a strange place, especially out in public. The unknown whereabouts of James the jerk made him nervous. His fingers tightened around the fork. Even though he knew better, he itched to throw a couple of good punches if the sleazeball decided to show his face in Whisper Falls.

"You own the ranch near the waterfall, don't you?" Davis Turner asked, interrupting his thoughts of revenge. "The pretty ranch that sets down in the valley."

Austin put his fork down and shifted slightly toward the other man. "That's my place. Have you been out my way?"

"The kids and I picnicked near the waterfall a few weeks ago. Paige would take a tent and move out there if I'd let her." The little girl grinned up at her dad. "Beautiful area."

"We like it. It's peaceful." Or it had been until the Whisper Falls madness began and a certain blonde whacked him upside the head.

His ears strained toward the closed office. What was taking her and Evelyn so long?

"You got a ranch?" Davis Turner's little boy eyed Austin's boots and hat with interest. "Do you have horses, too?"

Austin dipped his head at the eager face and a

mouth smeared with vanilla ice cream. "Sure do. You must like horses."

"Yes, but Daddy says you can't have a horse in town." The boy's disgust with this unfortunate turn of events was accented with a deep sigh.

"Sorry, buddy," Davis said, touching the boy lightly on the shoulder. "That's the way things are. Someday, maybe we'll buy some land in the country and you can have a horse all your own. Until then…" As if he'd suddenly come up with a solution, Davis looked to Austin. "You don't happen to give riding lessons, do you?"

The idea set Austin back. Riding lessons? "Never thought about it."

"Nathan's wanted a horse since he was big enough to talk." Davis wadded a paper napkin and placed it on the counter. "I'd be glad to pay if you'd be interested in teaching him."

"I don't know. I'll have to think on it," Austin said, more to be polite than because he was actually considering such an invasion of his privacy.

"With the influx of tourists a man could make good money with a stable of riding horses."

A shiver of dread ran through Austin. The last thing he wanted was more strangers traipsing around his land, poking into his business. "Not my kind of thing."

The affable Davis smiled as he lifted his drinking cup. "I understand. You did mention peace and quiet, something you won't get with kids around. But if you change your mind…" He reached inside his golf-style shirt pocket and handed Austin a business card.

"Sure, sure." Austin glanced at the card. "Ceramic tile? So you're a tile mason?"

"Showers, kitchens, floors. I should be working today, but school is out for a parent-teacher conference." He rattled the ice in his cup. "Being a single dad, I took off for that."

"And to hang out with your favorite kids, right, Daddy?" Paige batted long, pale lashes at her father.

He scuffed the top of her head. "Right."

Austin's gaze fell to the little boy. Nathan had gone from hopeful to deflated when Davis had asked about riding lessons. Austin's conscience niggled. What harm was there in giving one little kid a ride on a well-broke horse? On the other hand, he didn't want to get something started. Familiarity breeds contempt, and he'd had enough of that to last a lifetime. Still, Davis seemed like a good guy, and a boy who loved horses needed to learn somewhere.

Warring with himself, Austin returned to his pie and ice cream. He scooped a giant bite of ice cream and shoved the fork into his mouth. A powerful pain shot from the roof of his mouth to the top of his head. He dropped the fork and pressed a hand to each temple, certain his brain was about to explode.

"Uh-oh, brain freeze," the little girl said and hopped from her stool to stand beside Austin. "I'll pray for you." And she did.

When the moment passed, Austin shook his head to find the headache gone. No surprise there. An ice-cream headache came and went. The relief had nothing to do with prayer.

He shifted uncomfortably on the bar stool. All this company was starting to get under his skin. When Annalisa had entered the snack shop, she'd looked too pretty with her hair all fluffed up and glossy, and now some kid prayed for him while another looked at him with a mix of hero worship and disappointment. He should have stayed home.

But there was the matter of his unwanted houseguest who chose that moment to reappear from the back room, a dazed look on her face. Interestingly, she went behind the counter. Miss Evelyn, who'd followed her from the office, pulled an apron from a hook. "Let's see what you can manage with that hand of yours."

Miss Evelyn had hired her. Good. Fine. Perfect. Austin's responsibility ended here and now.

He readied once more to depart. As he stood, Annalisa looked his way.

"Austin, are you leaving?"

He cupped his hat in one hand, fingers wide

on the crown. Did she expect him to stick around and play bodyguard and listen to her chat up the smiley single guy with the two cute kids?

"Are you staying?"

"Evelyn's going to show me around." She pushed at her perfect hair. "I'm going to work here, starting tomorrow. Isn't that great?"

"Congratulations." Austin didn't see all that much to learn in the small snack bar, but her eyes were so sparkly and happy he wasn't going to rain on her parade.

"Thank you." She glanced at Miss Evelyn who was beaming like a proud mama.

"I'll see you later, then." He jammed his hat down on his head and turned to leave.

Evelyn's voice stopped him. "Don't run off, Austin Blackwell. We need to talk."

Austin pivoted. He'd almost forgotten that the Whisper Falls mastermind wanted to talk to him. Was he ever going to get out of here? Fingers circling the brim of his Stetson, he waited to hear what she'd say.

Miss Evelyn bustled toward him.

"Your sister is a fantastic advocate for Whisper Falls and always willing to lend a hand," she began.

"I'll tell her you said so."

Miss Evelyn parked her short, stocky self in his

circle of personal space and demanded, "When are you going to do *your* part?"

He blinked, frowning. "Pardon?"

"In a week or so, we're tearing down the old Rankin house and clearing off the mess of outbuildings and chicken coops in the back. The whole place is an eyesore and a danger. We need some men to do the heavy work."

Davis Turner, who'd been smiling at Annalisa as though she was the last apple on the tree, piped up. "You can add me to the list."

Miss Evelyn fairly beamed. So did Annalisa. In fact, the look she gave Davis was warm enough to melt chocolate.

"That's the spirit," said Miss Evelyn. "What about you, Austin? Surely, you can spare a day or two."

She'd put him on the spot, and he'd look like a horse's backside if he said no. Not that he minded the work. He just didn't want to get involved with a lot of nosy people.

"I guess I could."

Davis Turner's son slid from his bar stool. "Daddy said Mr. Blackwell should open a riding stable. Don't you think that's a great idea, Miss Evelyn?"

She clasped the boy by the shoulders, but her eyes were on Austin. "That's a marvelous idea, Nathan. Austin, you'd be good at that and you've got the land. Maybe you could open up an RV camp and guide trail rides. The council would print up a nice, colorful brochure and post it on the website." Evelyn was off on one of her brainstorms. "Horse lovers would flock to Whisper Falls like summer geese."

Exactly what he did not want. "Not interested. Too much liability." A good excuse even if it wasn't the real reason. "Let me know about the work day."

Once more he headed for the door. This time he safely made his escape.

Chapter Six

Annalisa found the cowboy in the horse barn, pitchforking clean straw into a stall. He must not have heard her come in, so she watched for a moment as the muscles in his broad back flexed with the rhythm of his work.

The dust and hay smell of the barn drew her back a few years to a happy time and place when life had not been so complicated. She could almost hear her grandpa humming "What a Friend We Have in Jesus" in a voice roughened by years of work in the Kansas wind and dust. Olivia had been there, too, riding the top of the gate, her double ponytails a frame for her oval face and brown eyes.

But that was before they'd burned all the bridges and left each other behind.

"Would you like some help?"

The pitchfork stopped moving as Austin swiveled to face her. Sweat beaded his forehead. Specks of straw rode his shoulders and black hair. He looked incredibly masculine, a ruggedly outdoorsy look that sent tiny needles of interest dancing along her skin.

"How did you get home?"

"Uncle Digger drove me."

"You should have called." He stabbed the pitchfork into the remaining pile of straw and left the tool standing straight as a new fence post.

Annalisa wasn't sure if he was angry or concerned.

"I didn't want to bother you. You've done enough."

"I forgot you didn't have a car." He frowned, his breath puffing from the exertion. "I should have stuck around."

She reached out, started to touch his arm, but changed her mind and let her hand fall to her side. "Don't look so guilty. I'm perfectly capable of taking care of myself."

He looked as if he didn't believe her, and for good reason. From the moment they'd met, she'd leaned on his good nature and done anything *except* take care of herself. But no more. Even though the snack shop pay was small, the job was a start. Somehow she'd get back on her feet and never have to depend on anyone, especially a man, again. She never wanted to be as vulnerable as she'd been that day at the waterfall.

"How did things go at the Iron Horse?"

His question surprised her. She hadn't expected him to care one way or the other. "Very well. The work is easy, and I have no problem as long as I don't have to lift anything."

"Uncle Digger can do the lifting."

"That's what he said." She smiled, relaxed a little. "Cassie was right. They're nice people. So are Davis Turner and his kids. She says they all attend the same church."

"Whisper Falls is kind of churchy, if that's a word." He ran the back of one arm over his damp forehead.

"I used to be like that." And she wanted to be again. Since that bizarre incident at the waterfall when Austin had showed up after she'd prayed, Annalisa had tried to refocus on God. Praying eased her anxiety and helped her sleep. Talking to Cassie, who had the faith of Abraham, eased her self-recriminations. Life was too hard without God to lean on. "Cassie invited me to church. Do you attend?"

"Nope." Abruptly, he jerked the pitchfork from the straw and jabbed a forkful, spreading the scent as well as the substance around the stall. She saw the stiffness in his body, heard the tension in his voice. Instinctively she knew. Like her, he'd stumbled somewhere along the muddy path of life.

She didn't ask, couldn't. But she wondered what had happened.

A wooden-handled rake leaned against one wall of the stall. She took it in hand much as she had the broom and began smoothing the straw.

"You don't have to do that."

"I know. I want to."

"Suit yourself." With a shrug he went back to work.

His wasn't the friendliest invitation she'd ever had, but it would do. At some point this morning, he'd lifted the three-day injunction. At least, she thought he had, and she wanted to pull her weight.

"I'll get an apartment as soon as I have the money saved."

Austin peered at her over his shoulder. "You're safer here."

Apparently, that was as much of a commitment as she was going to get. She'd take it. Gladly.

One of the horses, this one a tall buckskin with black mane, tail and stockings and an eggshell-colored body, ambled to the stall door and stuck her head inside.

"We have company."

Austin's head turned toward the fancy-looking mare. "Dixie's a pest. Thinks she's a dog." He stepped to the animal, wrapped an arm around her head and stroked her long face. "How you doing, pretty girl?"

The mare blew softly and licked her lips.

"She trusts you." Animals instinctively know, she thought.

Austin gave her a curious look. "You familiar with horses?"

"A little. Enough to know a horse is comfortable when she licks her lips."

He backed the mare into the open area of the barn. Annalisa set the rake aside to follow, watching his gentle way with the animal. He went to a fifty-gallon barrel, dipped in a hand and came out with a handful of cubes. The horse snuffled. Her ears flickered and she bobbed her big head until he offered the treat.

Yes, there was a lot of good in Austin Blackwell. At least, his animals thought so.

"I took you for a city girl," he said.

Annalisa ran her hand down the mare's sleek, warm neck. "I grew up in Wichita but spent summers on my grandpa's farm."

"So you're a Kansas farm girl."

Smiling softly, she pointed at him. "Don't say it."

"What?"

"We're not in Kansas anymore, Toto."

He huffed, expression amused. "I guess you've heard that a million times."

"You have no idea. Cassie said you moved here from Texas?"

Again, his face closed up tight and defensive. "Cassie talks too much."

He turned away from her, leading the horse toward the open pasture and several other horses. Annalisa knew she'd touched a sensitive nerve but didn't understand why. When Cassie had told her about Texas, she hadn't mentioned anything troubling. But clearly something about his Texas past had rubbed a blister on Austin's heart. Was that the reason he was such a loner?

"I didn't mean to pry," she said, and when he didn't respond, she shifted gears. "What did you think of Miss Evelyn's idea about a riding stable?"

"I didn't think about it at all."

"Davis Turner and his kids were wild about the idea."

Austin didn't respond immediately. He appeared to mull the comment while he slid a halter onto Dixie's head and latched the clasp. "What did you think of him?"

The question caught Annalisa off guard. "Who? Davis Turner?"

"Uh-huh."

Austin picked up one of the mare's feet and inspected her hoof. His head was bent so that the autumn sun gleamed off his dark hair, an iridescent spectrum of color. In the pasture beyond, one of the other horses whinnied and the mare answered.

"He seems nice. His kids were well-behaved and cute."

"He's single."

She stiffened. "What an odd thing to say. Am I supposed to care about that?"

Austin opened the gate, patted the horse's hip and turned her out. Head high and black mane flying, the mare galloped toward the others.

He shut the gate and leaned his forearms on the top rail, gazing out toward the mountains. "After what happened with the boyfriend, you need to be careful."

Was he accusing her of inviting trouble? Of flirting with a strange man?

Annalisa's hackles went up like porcupine quills. "People in Whisper Falls are friendly. To make friends, you have to be friendly, too. I'm lonely here, Austin. I want to get to know people." She slapped her hand atop the iron railing. The sound echoed like a gunshot and startled a nearby crow into flight. One of the dogs, asleep in the sun next to the barn, raised his head in curiosity. "Let me be very clear about one thing. I just escaped a horrible, controlling relationship. If I never get involved with another man, it will be too soon. Davis Turner seems like a nice man, and that's all I have to say."

"Didn't mean to get you all twisted up." With deliberate ease Austin turned his rugged face in her direction and stared long enough that Annalisa squirmed beneath his scrutiny. After a minute, he turned back to the gate, propped a boot on the bottom rail and motioned toward the mountains. "Whisper Falls is beautiful this time of year. I figure you didn't notice much that first day, you being hurt and all. If you're up for the trip, I'll saddle a couple of horses and we can ride."

Annalisa felt off balance as if she'd missed part of the conversation. One minute she was spouting off in blistering terms and the next she was considering a pleasant horseback ride in the color-splashed forest.

"I'd love to, but my arm—" she raised the green cast.

The corners of Austin's mouth tipped up as he swiveled his head in her direction. "You only need one. The horses do the rest."

"Well, I…" She stopped and cocked her head to one side. "You're a strange man, Austin Blackwell."

He snorted. "That's not the first time I've heard that. You want to ride or not?"

They squared off at each other like two prize fighters. Annalisa didn't know whether to laugh or run. Deciding she'd done enough running, she said, "I do."

As if the matter was of great importance, Austin's shoulders relaxed. He dusted his hat against his jeans and said, "All right, then. Let's go."

They rode along in silence at first, the Indian summer sun warm and relaxing. Austin didn't know what had come over him but when Annalisa had feathered up like a mad hen, he'd wanted to laugh and kiss her. Lord help him, he hadn't wanted to kiss a woman in—well, in a long time. His was a silly reaction and one precipitated by having a pretty, vulnerable woman underfoot again. Cassie was pretty, but she was his sister and certainly not vulnerable. She'd take a man's knees out if he messed with her. Annalisa, on the other hand, worried him.

He shot a glance at the blonde riding at his side on Blaze, the gentlest horse on the ranch. "You've ridden before."

"Plenty of times."

"Let me guess. Grandpa's farm?"

"Right." She smiled and he noticed the slight overbite that enhanced rather than detracted from her appeal. Contrary to what he'd thought the first time he'd seen her, Annalisa Keller wasn't picture-perfect or overly sophisticated. She was real. Like Miss Evelyn said, she had good eyes. Real good eyes.

"Granddads are special."

"Mine was. He was my mother's father, and

basically the only dad my sister and I ever knew. That's why we spent summers with him. Well, that and my mother's job. She sent us to Grandpa Sims's to keep us out of mischief while she was working."

"Did it?"

"Keep us out of mischief?" She shrugged. "Most of the time Grandpa kept us busy, but when we got older we were probably a handful."

"Teenage girls," he said with a rueful shake of his head.

"Girls? What are you talking about?" She replied in mock offense. "Boys are the ones who caused all the trouble!"

He laughed at that one. He could just imagine Annalisa and her sister drawing a crowd. Which turned his thoughts back to the snack shop and Davis Turner. She'd claimed no interest in the man even though Davis had certainly perked up when she'd arrived. Not that Austin cared one way or the other about her relationships except for the uncomfortable feeling that he was responsible for her.

"What about you?" she asked. "Were you close to your grandparents?"

"My dad's parents, Grandpa and Grandma Blackwell. They owned the family ranch where I grew up. In fact, this land was once theirs. I bought it after Grandpa passed on."

"Any siblings other than Cassie?"

"Nope. One is enough." But he grinned when he said it.

"She's awesome. I'm so glad we met." The sun went behind a cloud and she swallowed, her slim throat flexing. "Not the *way* we met, but I'm happy to know her."

"What about you? Any siblings other than the troublesome Olivia?"

Her glance fell to the saddle horn where she rested the awkward, heavy cast. In a quiet voice, she said, "All my family is gone now. Even Olivia."

Compassion pinched his chest. She had no one, no one at all, not even the sister she'd obviously adored. He considered asking what had happened but refrained. His questions would lead to questions from her, and he had no intentions of discussing Blair with anyone.

The horses' heads bobbed lower as the incline increased and they plodded higher. Austin tilted forward to ease the strain.

One gloved hand holding the reins, he motioned with the other. "Around this bend, you can see where the river starts its descent into the valley."

"Does the river flow on your property?"

"Along the back edge to the south."

When they crested the bend, he heard her swift intake of breath, the awed murmur of pleasure at the sight spreading below and beyond. Her reaction filled him with a sense of rightness. He'd wanted her to appreciate the view the way he did.

He pulled Cisco to a stop, leaning forward to pat the dependable gelding's neck. "Pretty, isn't it?"

As far as the eye could see, a dappled carpet of brilliant reds, oranges, yellows and greens in every shade undulated over the low, rounded mountains. Down below, in a narrow valley the river was a silver ribbon edged with yellow blossoms—black-eyed Susans, Cassie had told him.

Annalisa shifted toward him with an expression of awe. "Austin, this is glorious."

"Like it?" He knew she did, but he wanted to hear her say the words, wanted an excuse to watch the pleasure move across her face.

She drank in the panorama, as if her soul was parched and nature's coat of many colors had the power to refresh. He understood. He'd come here when despair had threatened to overwhelm and no help was in sight.

"God does such good work," she breathed.

For a second, he wanted to agree but stubbornly held back. He and God weren't on speaking terms anymore. The spot below his rib, where his soul resided felt as hollow as a rotten log.

He lifted an arm to point. "Look."

Blue eyes, made more vivid by a matching sky, followed the direction of his aim. A red-tailed hawk, wings spread wide, glided gracefully over the valley in search of prey.

"What a gorgeous sight."

"Yep," he agreed, settling into his self-imposed role of tour guide. "Bald eagles winter near here, too. Now, that's something to see. Huge birds. Wings six-feet wide, and yet they fly with grace and ease. Majestic."

"Other than on television, I've never seen a bald eagle."

"We'll have to remedy that." Austin didn't know why he was making promises. By winter, Annalisa would be tired of living in the sticks and eager to make her escape. He hoped she wasn't foolish enough to run back to James. "Ready to head to the house? Cassie will be home soon."

Annalisa stretched in the stirrups and rotated her shoulders. "I am a little tired."

"Tenderfoot," he teased.

"It's not my *feet* that are tender."

Her answer tickled him so much that he threw his head back and laughed. The sound echoed down into the valley and ricocheted off the mountain. Annalisa giggled, a cute feminine sound that filled his chest with warm pleasure.

With a click of his tongue, he turned the horses around, and they started down the mountain. Along the way, Annalisa exclaimed over every flower, every scamper of lizard or squirrel into the dry leaves. Her enthusiasm both amused and buoyed him.

"This was fun, Austin, and relaxing, too," she said as they rode into the barnyard. "I'd forgotten how much I love being outdoors in nature. Thank you."

"Anytime." And he meant it. The afternoon with Annalisa, seeing the Ozarks through her eyes, had refreshed him, maybe more than it had her. He'd missed the pleasant camaraderie of sharing the outdoors with someone equally as enthralled. And she had been. He could tell by the sparkle in her eyes and the flush of fresh air on her perfect complexion.

"You're a great tour guide."

"Don't mention tourists," he said, teasing but serious, too.

"So I guess a riding stable is out of the question?" she teased in return.

"Absolutely." This time he didn't tease.

"What about Davis's little boy? He would have loved riding the way we did, don't you agree?"

Davis again. Leather squeaking, Austin dismounted, his good mood evaporating.

"You think I should invite him out?"

"I don't know. I remember how much I loved horses when I was a little girl. Still do. It's a bond you never forget."

He knew better than most about the bond between humans and animals. His horses and dogs kept him sane.

"I don't want strangers poking around." He also didn't want nonstrangers like Davis Turner getting up close and personal.

Annalisa gripped the saddle horn with her good hand as if to dismount.

"Hold on," he said, glad for an excuse to change the subject. "I'll get you."

She had already started the descent, awkward with casted arm in the way. When Austin caught her around the waist, her full body weight caught him off balance. He staggered backward a couple of steps but held on and eased her to a stand. They were close enough that he smelled apple shampoo and the essence of autumn leaves. He gripped her waist with both hands and steadied her. She looked up, eyes wide and shining and as blue as the sky above.

A flash of yearning came again. To pull her close and hold her. Maybe to kiss her.

As if the touch of her skin burned, he abruptly released her.

Something was going on here, and he didn't quite know what to do about it. "I'll unsaddle the horses. You go on to the house."

"I can help. I don't mind."

He clamped his jaw tight. "I do. Now go."

* * *

Austin Blackwell was the most complicated man she'd ever met. One minute, he was sweet as sugar and the next, he'd bare his teeth, ready to bite.

"What's with your brother?" she asked. She'd left Austin, at his rather unfriendly insistence, to care for the animals and was now inside the house with Cassie. True to form, Cassie had arrived with a double cheese pizza supreme and a big bottle of cola. How the woman remained trim on a steady diet of fast food remained a mystery.

Eyebrows raised in question, Cassie set three plates on the table. "Why? What did he do now?"

Annalisa told her about the unexpectedly lovely ride and then his sudden crankiness. "I don't know if he likes me or finds me a nuisance."

Cassie's musical laugh danced around the pleasant kitchen. "Both. Girl, don't you get it? He likes you a lot and his feelings scare him silly."

"You think so?" The idea came as a complete surprise. Austin liked her? And his feelings scared him? She couldn't imagine the big cowboy being afraid of anything except tourists. Certainly not of her.

"I know so. Austin's been nothing short of a recluse since Blair's death, and now you've gotten his blood circulating again. He doesn't know what to do about you."

Hand on the cabinet door, Annalisa paused. "Who's Blair?"

"Oops, there goes my big mouth again." Cassie took a head of lettuce out of the refrigerator. "You probably want a salad with the pizza, don't you?"

Annalisa took the lettuce and placed it on the counter. "Was she an old girlfriend who broke his heart?"

An unrequited love would explain a lot about his gruff behavior.

Cassie seemed to consider as she took three glasses from the cabinet and set them on the countertop. She glanced at the back door. Austin was nowhere in sight.

"Okay. You told me about your ex, so I suppose it's only fair. Blair was his wife. She died."

Annalisa's hand went to her mouth. "I am so sorry. How awful. What happened?"

Poor Austin. No wonder he kept to himself. He was a grieving widower.

Austin's sister gnawed at her bottom lip, brow furrowed. "Look, Annalisa, Austin is really, really closed-mouthed about Blair. Her death was…odd, and Austin was almost destroyed when it happened. I should not have brought up the subject. If he wants you to know, he should be the one to tell you." She reached out to grip Annalisa's fingers. Her touch was cold. "Don't say anything, okay?"

"Okay." But a dozen questions tumbled through her head.

What had happened to Austin's wife?

Chapter Seven

Austin was home alone. At last.

The girls, as he thought of them, had gone to work this morning as usual. Annalisa seemed to be settling in to her job and making friends, and Cassie had drawn the newcomer into the town hullabaloo. In fact, she and Cassie, along with Miss Evelyn, had warned him he was expected at the next cleanup site.

He walked through the house, bewildered to be restless, maybe a tad lonely. He who preferred solitude, missed the quiet conversation and activity of a certain woman.

Tootsie tapped along beside him, occasionally cocking her head as if to say, "What's wrong with you?"

"Good question," he said.

He felt itchy, uncomfortable, had a twist in his gut for some reason.

Usually, the ranch kept him busy, but today he felt at loose ends. He had fence to fix and plenty to do, but he couldn't get off high center.

He paused at the guest room. The door was open and he could see inside the room now occupied by Annalisa Keller.

She was doing okay. He didn't need to worry about her. But he did. In odd moments, when he least expected it, he relived a flash of that first day, of her fear and brokenness. Even though bruises faded and bones healed, he hadn't forgotten.

But Annalisa was plucky, a fighter. That's why she'd survived and why she was here in the Ozarks instead of in California with that abusive jerk of a boyfriend.

Last night, the three of them had sat on the porch while frogs croaked, whippoorwills called and the Ozark air grew chilly. Cassie had filled them in on the happenings in town, although Annalisa now came home with stories of her own.

He thought about the way she'd giggled when Cassie related the story of Evangeline Perryman's prize pig. Evangeline had brought the swine into the beauty shop for a pedicure, and Cassie herself had painted the hog's toenails—hot pink with French tips.

He'd wondered if Cassie told the whole truth, but the story had given them all a good laugh, so he supposed it didn't matter.

Annalisa had said something about looking for an apartment soon which he'd decided was for the best. She couldn't stay at the remote ranch forever and was probably eager to get back to civilization.

The thought left a hollow feeling in his gut.

The telephone rang and he pushed off the edge of the door facing. Tootsie trailed him to the kitchen phone.

"Hello."

There was a pause on the other end. Telemarketer, he thought with irritation, but before he could hang up, a male voice said, "Annalisa Keller, please."

Austin's grip tightened on the receiver. Annalisa hadn't mentioned giving his number to anyone. "Who is this?"

Another pause and then, "A friend of hers. It's urgent I speak with her. Is she there?"

Austin scowled, his mind playing ping-pong with the possibilities. Who knew she was here? And how did anyone other than townsfolk who would give their names obtain that information? "No, she isn't."

"Is this Blackwell?"

The hair prickled on Austin's arms. "Who's asking?"

"I understand she's been staying with you since her accident. I hope she's recovering."

At the mention of Annalisa's "accident," a shiver snaked up Austin's neck. "She's fine."

"Glad to hear it." An intake of breath. "I know she's there. Put her on the phone. I have something important to tell her. An emergency of sorts."

The man's pushiness was starting to grate on Austin's nerves. If a true emergency existed, why didn't he explain?

"She's at work. Who is this? And how did you get my phone number?"

"Annalisa has a job?" The man sounded surprised. "Where?"

"Look, buddy, if you're a friend of Annalisa, you would know that. Leave your name and number, and I'll tell her you called."

"Never mind. That won't be necessary. Thank you for your time."

A click sounded in Austin's ear.

He scowled at the receiver before hanging it up. "Weird. Real weird."

Telemarketers grew cleverer all the time, but this caller had known too much. Austin grasped the receiver again and pressed caller ID. His heart fell to the tips of his boot. The warning voice in his head had been correct.

No name, but a California number.

On the drive into town, Austin tried unsuccessfully to convince himself that the number could have been a telemarketer in California. Yet, he knew better. A telemarketer would not have known about Annalisa's accident.

He burst through the door of the Iron Horse Snack Shop like a steer out of a roping chute. A half dozen customers swiveled to take in the newcomer, raised a hand in greeting or nodded, before returning to their food, drink and conversations.

Behind the counter, Annalisa was arranging tortilla chips into a paper bowl. When she saw him, she flashed a smile. "Austin, hi. What are you doing here?"

He charged up to the counter and leaned in. "Are you okay?"

Expression puzzled, she said, "I'm great. Is something wrong?"

Deep breath, Blackwell. Don't scare her to death.

In his rush to get here, he'd not considered exactly what to tell her or how much. Her old boyfriend had done a number on her sense of safety and the last thing he wanted to do was upset her again. For days after he'd found her at Whisper Falls, she'd been skittish and nervous. She had checked and rechecked windows and doors at night, jumped at every noise. Only in the past couple of days had she begun to relax, and he wanted her to stay that way.

But he was here and had to tell her something.

"I was just wondering about—" his attention went to her cast "—your arm. I mean, how are you handling the workload? Is it too much for you? You don't have to work here if it's too hard. You can stay at the ranch, work for me."

He liked the idea immediately although he wasn't sure where it had come from. Having Annalisa on the ranch all the time made perfect sense. He would be there with her. He could keep her safe.

Annalisa looked at him as if he'd grown an extra eye.

"I've worked here for over a week, Austin. Everything is great." She set the nacho bowl on the counter, and then with one hand, she poured a dipper of hot cheese sauce over the chips. "Are you sure nothing's wrong?"

"I could pay you more than you make here."

"To do what? Feed the dogs?" She spooned a pile of sliced jalapeños over the cheese.

"And cook. Cassie is starving me to death. You could be our housekeeper, cook, whatever you want."

Annalisa was already shaking her head. "You and Cassie have done enough, Austin. I can't impose on you any more than I already have."

"It's no imposition." His voice rose a little. She didn't get the point and he couldn't tell her.

"I like working here. Whisper Falls people are

warm and embracing, and I'm making friends. But thank you for the offer."

"Oh. Right." He got the message. No sensible, attractive female wanted to be stuck out in the sticks with a cranky cowboy and a pack of dogs. Women need a social life. Hadn't he learned anything from Blair? "Just an idea. If you change your mind…"

With deft, one-handed skill, she slid the nachos in front of a pimple-faced teenage boy, adding a smile for good measure. "Would you like something to drink with that?"

The skinny kid hitched a shoulder. "Dew."

"Large?"

"Yeah."

While she completed the boy's order, Austin brooded over his choices. She was a grown woman, and he had no right keeping this information from her. On the other hand, he wasn't positive James had been the caller. Why upset her for nothing?

Austin watched as she served up the boy's drink and said something that made the sulky teenager smile. Another customer lifted his coffee cup and she spouted off a teasing remark as she whipped the carafe from the stand. She looked happy. In the past few days, a sparkle had come into her eyes and the jittery worry had receded.

Hands on his hips, Austin tilted his head back

to watch the ceiling fans spin in slow circles. He couldn't do it. He could not say the words that would put fear back into her life.

"Here he comes again." Miss Evelyn nudged Annalisa as Austin sauntered through the door of the snack shop.

"He likes your pie."

Miss Evelyn laughed so hard that Annalisa had to pound her on the back.

"Shh," she whispered, giggling. Miss Evelyn was right. Austin had been in the shop every afternoon for more than a week. And every time he passed through the doors, hat in hand and dark hair mussed, her heart did a silly little jitterbug.

"You okay?" he asked as he always did.

"Fine. What brings you to town?"

"Got hungry for Miss Evelyn's apple pie."

Behind her, Evelyn broke into another fit of laughter. Her eyes watered. When Austin stared at the rosy-cheeked woman, she waved a plump hand. "Private joke. I gotta run. Ladies Auxiliary meeting at the church." To Annalisa, she said, "Get him that pie, hon."

Then she laughed all the way out the door.

Austin slung one leg over the bar stool. He wasn't stupid. He knew why Miss Evelyn was cackling like a hen. She thought he'd developed a crush on Annalisa. He plopped his hat on the stool next to him and ran a hand through his mussed hair. Making the daily trip to town cost him some work time at the ranch, but the peace of mind was worth the effort. Today, the rain was excuse enough.

"Place is kind of empty," he said, circling the room with a glance as Annalisa slid the white saucer of pie in front of him.

"Uncle Digger left with a trainload of customers a few minutes ago."

"I thought it might be the rain."

"Could be. Business has been slower than usual."

"Sit down and I'll buy you something to eat."

"Okay." She glanced at the big clock on the back wall. "Cassie's coming by at three to drive me to Dr. Ron's."

"Are you sick?"

She indicated the cast. "He's putting on a short, waterproof version. I'll actually be able to move my elbow again." She lifted both arms—as much as possible—in a victory shake. "Cannot wait for that!"

"A cause for celebration. Bring more pie."

With a smile, she opened the refrigerator and brought a yogurt cup loaded with fresh fruit to the counter. "You have pie. I'll have this. Cassie's fast food diet is wearing me down."

"Another reason to hire on as my cook."

Not taking the bait, Annalisa settled in beside him with her snack, and he caught the smell of French fries and strawberries mingled with her shampoo—some fancy, girly stuff Cassie had brought home from the beauty shop. He let the scent settle in his lungs right next to the apple and cinnamon.

"So what's new in Whisper Falls today?" He cut a sliver of flaky, soft crust. After eating the dessert every day for over a week, he wasn't quite as eager for the first bite. Maybe he should try something else tomorrow.

"Everyone's talking about Pumpkin Fest and the beautification project." Her spoon did a slow swirl around the fluffy yogurt. "Are you going?"

"Never have."

"Never?"

"I don't see the point." A flicker in blue irises told him she was disappointed by his response. He didn't want to disappoint her, but… "You should go. Cassie makes a big deal of it."

"She has a date."

The news shocked him to the toes of his Tony Lamas. "She does? With who?"

"Rusty Fairchild."

"The mayor?" He couldn't believe it. The baby-faced mayor couldn't be more than twenty-five.

From all appearances, he didn't even shave! "He's too young for her."

"Why, Austin Blackwell, you silly man. Cassie isn't yet thirty, and she's pretty and sweet and loads of fun. The mayor is fortunate she said yes."

"I just never thought—" He bit off the words. Cassie had been devastated to lose Darrell.

Annalisa touched the back of his hand. "Cassie is healing, Austin. She has an enormous capacity to love. Keeping it bottled inside isn't good for her."

As if his hand had a mind of its own, it turned palm up so Annalisa's fingers rested lightly in the center. He was tempted to close his fingers and hold on. Tempted, but he didn't. "It's too soon."

She stared, gaze pinned to his. "Are you talking about her or yourself?"

The question startled him. He withdrew his hand, fisting it tight against the edge of the counter. Had his ever-meddling sister said something? "What do you mean?"

Annalisa shook her head and the overhead light picked up the shine of her golden hair. "I was thinking of the way I feel, I suppose. Part of me wants to hide away from life and never get involved again. I'm afraid of getting hurt, of making more mistakes, but that's not living." She picked at the stem of a fresh strawberry. "Jesus came that we might have an abundant life, free from fear and worry. Uncle Digger told me that. I don't think I'd ever heard it before."

Had he? He didn't think so.

"I want my life to be full, Austin, full of love and laughter and family. Don't you want that, too?"

The conversation was getting way too complicated for him. "All I want is a successful ranch and this piece of pie."

But he lied. He wanted a lot more than that. So much that he couldn't meet her eyes again as he sat like a tree stump, contemplating her wise comments.

His life was good, full. Sort of. Just because he didn't join every committee in the Ozarks like his sister didn't mean squat. He'd always thought Cassie volunteered to fill the hole left by her shattered future. Maybe she did. But a date? With a mayor who looked like Mayberry's Opie?

"Customers," Annalisa said, pushing away from her seat.

Austin recognized Creed Carter's trim, military build and aviator sunglasses and the ever-present black T-shirt with the chopper logo. The man was pleasant enough, but sheesh, the noise from that helicopter. Austin hated it.

"How ya doing, Austin?" Creed joined him at the bar.

"Good. Yourself?"

"Can't complain."

"What can I get for you, Creed?" Annalisa had returned to her place behind the bar.

"Got any salad?"

"We made some fresh this morning. Would you like grilled chicken on it as usual?"

As usual? How often did the chopper pilot come in here?

"Yes, thanks." Creed motioned toward the glass-fronted box filled with a variety of bottled drinks. "A bottle of OJ, too."

Salad? Orange juice? What was this guy, a health food nut? Whatever happened to men who liked fat, greasy burgers and sugar-laden soda pop? Men like him?

"I guess you can't fly much on rainy days," Annalisa said as she neatly arranged two microwaved chicken strips atop a bowl of crisp lettuce and tomatoes.

"Going up is not the problem, but as a general rule tourists don't get out in weather like this. Have you ever been up in a chopper?"

"Never. It must be fun."

"Flying's more than fun." The guy's swarthy face glowed like a kid's on Christmas. "You have God and Heaven above you and all creation below. There's no place else I'd rather be."

Austin wished good old Creed was up there right now. Him and his good looks and easy conversation. Austin searched for something to say and came up short. The pilot, on the other hand, was as chatty as Mickey Mouse.

Austin didn't figure he should be surprised. Since Annalisa started working at the Iron Horse, yahoos like Davis Turner and the chopper pilot seemed to show up every afternoon. Like bees to a bright flower, they came.

Austin scowled at his half-eaten pie.

"The flying business is slow today. Why don't you go up with me when you get off work?" Creed said. "I'll show you the Ozarks as you've never seen them."

"I'd love to." Her sparkly gaze flicked toward Austin. "Wouldn't that be fun?"

Surprised at how vehemently he objected, Austin found his voice. "You have a doctor's appointment."

"Oh, that's right. Rain check?" she asked, hopefully.

Creed's suntanned cheeks stretched wide. Enough white teeth to please an orthodontist flashed. "Done. Anytime you're ready, say the word and I'll take you flying."

Austin chased the pie with a swig of milk. It curdled in his stomach.

Chapter Eight

The next Saturday Austin found himself working beside Davis Turner and several other men as they ripped boards from the side of a dilapidated house and stacked them into piles. Whisper Falls was an old town and there were too many homes like this one that had fallen on hard times and were scheduled for demolition. In Whisper Falls, demolition wasn't a machine. It was a handful of volunteers rounded up by the venerable Evelyn Parsons.

Miss Evelyn strutted around the cluttered worksite like a banty rooster, handing out advice and encouragement while Annalisa, Cassie and others he knew mostly by name stuffed random garbage into black plastic trash bags. The day had the atmosphere and mood of a picnic rather than a lot of hard, dirty work. People joked and talked. Someone had brought an old boom box and cranked up some bluegrass music. And Miss Evelyn's committee promised food and drink.

The flyboy was there, too. Austin was still trying to decide if Creed had been hitting on Annalisa that day at the Iron Horse or if he was simply an outgoing, affable guy. So far, the two had paid little attention to each other and Annalisa hadn't taken him up on the offer to fly over the Ozarks. For some inexplicable reason Austin felt better knowing that.

The mysterious caller hadn't phoned again, either, and Austin figured he could lighten up on the daily guard duty. Maybe the call *had* been a telemarketer, not James, and he'd done the right thing by not telling Annalisa.

He breathed a sigh of relief. Perhaps James was gone for good, although a spot way down in the bottom of his gut remained unsettled. He knew about abusive men, control freaks who wanted to dominate women. They left their mark, both physically and mentally. Sometimes those marks never healed no matter how hard a good man tried.

At that moment, Annalisa and her oversize garbage bag rounded the corner of the house. His mouth went dry. Trying not to stare, even though that was exactly what he was doing, he casually tossed a broken board into the pile. She was wearing an ancient pair of Cassie's blue jeans, rolled at the ankle to compensate for the fact that she was taller than his sister. Her shirt was one of his old ones, tied at the curve of a slender waist. With her golden hair slicked up in a high, bouncy ponytail, she reminded him of girls in the old movie *Grease*. Cute. Gorgeous. Seriously hot. At that moment, with the morning sun heating the back of his neck and his heart thudding, he realized what he'd been denying for days. His daily treks to the Iron Horse and his evenings on the front porch listening to Annalisa's day were not completely about protecting her.

After six years of guarding his heart, he was in trouble, and he didn't know what to do about it.

"There's water and pop when you boys get thirsty," Miss Evelyn yelled, pointing toward a huge red ice chest in the back of a pickup truck. "Marvin is bringing sandwiches from the diner around noon."

Marvin Clemson owned a small café on Easy Street.

"What about you, cowboy?" Annalisa came toward him, smiling. "Want a soda? I'm parched."

"Water sounds good." He sleeved the sweat off his forehead, willing his pulse to settle. No use getting crazy. "How about you, Davis? Ready for a break?"

Davis tossed a board onto the pile. Dust puffed up and out. "Might as well. You buying?"

Austin grinned at the joke. "Sure. You can buy the next round."

With the ease of friends, an ease that surprised Austin no little amount, the men moved toward the truck. Annalisa fell in step next to Austin. Her positioning did not go unnoticed by the cowboy. A buzz of energy surged through his veins.

"We're getting a lot done," she said. "You guys are like a machine."

Austin removed his gloves and hung them on his back pocket. "That's because men love to tear up stuff. Putting it back together is the hard part."

"Ain't it the truth," Davis added, shaking his head in mock despair.

The more Austin worked beside him, the more he liked Davis Turner. He was witty, a hard worker and knew construction work like the palm of his hand. A Christian, too, but his frequent comments about God didn't bother Austin. Maybe Annalisa was getting to him on that count, too. Her quiet determination to set things right with God and herself touched him. He was still puzzled at how a woman of her intellect and strength could have ever gotten caught up in a relationship with an abuser. Maybe he would ask her sometime.

Davis reached the ice chest first and handed around bottles of cold water. Austin unscrewed the lid and downed half of his. Annalisa hopped up on the lowered tailgate to sip at hers. Feet swinging, she daintily wiped the condensation on her jeans. Austin rubbed his across the back of his neck, relishing the cold.

"How long do you think this job will take?" Annalisa asked.

"From start to finish?" Davis hiked an elbow on top of the pickup bed as he let the half-empty bottle dangle from long fingers. "We should be finished by late afternoon. Getting the old house down is one thing, but then we'll need to load the trash and wood, rake up the nails, run the weed eater."

"I have a feeling my whole body will hurt by sundown." Annalisa rotated her neck. A bone popped.

Austin laughed. He resisted the urge to rub the back of her neck. "It will. Like riding a horse all day, you'll feel every muscle tomorrow."

"At least I have both arms now. Sort of." She flexed her elbow. The new cast, a hot pink, was small, light and came only a few inches above her wrist. "I feel invincible."

But the cast was a reminder that she wasn't. That someone out there had hurt her and maybe would again if given the chance. Austin's jaw tightened. No one was going to hurt Annalisa. Not if he had anything to say about it.

"You look intense."

Annalisa's quiet voice brought him back to the moment.

"Sorry. Thinking."

"Should I ask?"

Davis spoke up. "Never ask a man what he's thinking. We're basically clueless."

Annalisa laughed, engaged in some light banter with Davis and Austin was off the hook.

He owed Davis one.

Directly in front of the pickup truck, Austin spied Miss Evelyn. Bent low into the backseat of an enormous 1980s model Lincoln Town Car, she came out waving a huge plastic zip-bag of cookies. With a voice that could be heard over Uncle Digger's passenger train, she hollered, "You kids want some of Miss Evelyn's homemade chocolate-chip cookies?"

A half dozen children, there with their parents, raced toward her like wild rabbits.

"Hey, what about us big boys?" Davis called. "Don't we deserve cookies?"

Davis's child, Nathan, spun around. "I'll share with you, Daddy."

Austin witnessed the sweet consideration of Davis's son with a nagging conscience. Not only did Nathan offer to share with his dad, but he also didn't push or shove in the line of kids; he actually waited his turn along with his sister. Davis had taught them well. They were nice children.

He also supposed they wouldn't cause any problems at the ranch. Giving the boy a ride or two wasn't that big a deal.

"You have good kids."

The big, sunny smile spread across Davis's work-flushed face. "I think so, but any dad likes to hear a compliment from someone else. Thanks." He downed the rest of his water and tossed the bottle into the trash bag Annalisa had hefted onto the tailgate. "Ready to get back to work?"

"Might as well." Without thinking about the action, Austin offered Annalisa a hand down from the tailgate. She hopped lightly to the ground, landing inches from his chest. Having her close was…nice. Torturous, but pleasant. Too bad neither of them was ready for a relationship. He didn't figure he ever would be.

"There's plenty of trash over our way," he said.

Her mouth curved upward. She reached for a new bag from the giant container in the back of the truck. "Trash Girl is on her way."

"Trash Girl? Is that a new comic book hero?"

"Haven't you heard? Annalisa by day. Trash Girl by night." Eyes dancing, she flexed a muscle. "Saving the environment from litter and other smelly things."

Davis joined the fun. "I hate to burst your bubble, Trash Girl, but it's broad daylight."

"Oh, rats." She snapped her fingers. "You're right. I've blown my disguise."

Yes, and she was blowing all his resistance right out of the water.

Feeling light and easy, the trio returned to the rapidly disappearing shell of a house. Annalisa donned a pair of rubber gloves and began picking up debris while the men went back to ripping boards.

Still, Austin couldn't get Davis's sweet son out of his head. He wanted to. He just couldn't. Finally, he said to Davis, "I was thinking..."

He shoved the claw of a hammer behind a rotted board and yanked. The resulting screech of nails and snap of old wood momentarily drowned out the conversation. Dust and wood chips spewed, polluting the air. A flurry of bugs swarmed upward. Austin shook his head and stepped back to breathe. "Whew, nasty stuff."

"No wonder the place is in such bad shape. Termites." Davis jammed a work boot against the side of the structure while loosening a window frame. "Sorry, I missed what you were saying."

"I was just thinking about your boy."

Davis paused and turned his quiet gaze on Austin. "Yeah? What about him?"

"Is he still asking about horses?"

"Practically every day. Why?"

"I've got a couple of good broke geldings. Dog

gentle." He huffed out an ironic laugh. "Creed's chopper doesn't even scare them. They're perfect for a first ride. Bring Nathan out to the ranch sometime."

A wide smile spread across Davis's affable face. "Any specific day better for you?"

"Nah, just give me a call."

Davis whipped a cell phone from his pocket. "What's your number?" Austin told him. He jabbed the information into the cell before pocketing it. "I can't wait to tell Nathan. He'll go crazy." He hitched a chin toward the little boy. "Do you mind?"

"Go ahead."

As Davis walked away, Annalisa tossed a handful of dirty paper into her sack and said, "That was incredibly kind, Austin."

"No big deal." He yanked at a rotted board, found the wood stronger than he'd suspected.

"Yes, it was. I know how you feel about your privacy."

He paused. "Do you?"

"I think I do. For some reason, people make you uncomfortable. Your ranch is your refuge."

Her assessment was right on target. Austin put his discomfort into the stubborn board and yanked with all his strength. When the board gave, he stumbled back, lost his footing and landed on his backside.

The fall jarred his teeth and knocked the wind out of him. Dust flew around his head. Coughing, he removed his hat and fanned. Before the dust could clear, Annalisa was beside him, holding back a laugh, eyes twinkling as she managed to ask, "Are you okay?"

Work around them had stopped. Only the whine of the boom box playing "Rolling in My Sweet Baby's Arms" broke the sudden pause in activity. Austin's sense of the ridiculous, something he'd considered long dead, heard the words of the song just as Annalisa offered a helping hand. Everything in him wanted to yank her down onto his lap.

Her gloved hand touched his. He wrapped his fingers around her wrist, fighting the urge. By now, the onlookers had released a collective breath and laughter floated over him. His eyes met Annalisa's twinkling blue ones.

He squinted playfully. "Are you laughing at me, Trash Girl?"

"Well, yes." She giggled, a musical sound that warmed the lining of his chest. "A cowboy in the dirt is a funny sight."

The urge became too strong.

With an answering snort, he tugged and brought her toppling down.

At first, she was stunned, but then Annalisa began to laugh harder than she had in a long time.

Austin was sitting amid a pile of dirt and trash, long, jean-clad legs stretched out before him and covered in dust. She had fallen across him like a downed tree, though his muscular cowboy body had taken the brunt of the impact.

"Hey, what's going on over here?" Austin's sister charged toward the fallen pair, black ponytail flapping beneath a bright yellow ball cap.

With mock anger, she slammed fists onto the waist of now filthy sweatpants. "Are you taking advantage of my brother?"

Heat suffused Annalisa's cheeks but knowing Cassie joked, she shot back, "I'm trying to, but he won't cooperate."

"Just like a man." Cassie pulled her to a stand, and they both reached back to help Austin. He got to his feet and shook like a dog, sending dust into the air again with intentional mischief.

"If you women are going to mistreat me, I'm going back to work." He stalked off a few feet before pivoting to declare, "No girls allowed. Just us guys."

Cassie stuck her tongue out at him. "Dream on, cowboy. We are women. We go where we want, do what we want. Right, Annalisa?"

She slapped Annalisa on the shoulder.

"Yeah! That's right." Annalisa thumbed her nose for good measure and was rewarded when

Austin shot her a hard-eyed squint before he laughed again.

"Women," he said, shaking his head in mock disgust before retrieving his crowbar and rejoining Davis and Creed. She could hear the men's good-natured ribbing as they got back to work.

"I've never seen this playful side of Austin," Annalisa said. "He's different today. Friendlier, funnier and definitely more playful."

"Getting out with friends is good for him, whether he knows it or not." Cassie slung an arm around Annalisa's shoulders. "*You're* good for him."

"Me?"

"Yes, you. He's been different ever since the day you arrived. He's falling for you, Annalisa."

Annalisa's stomach wobbled. A mix of dismay and pleasure warred inside. "Do you really think so?"

"I know my brother." Cassie dropped the arm to her side and faced Annalisa with a serious expression. "He's been through some stuff. Some bad stuff. For all his cowboy bluster, he's a softie."

Annalisa considered the way he was with his horses and dogs, the kindness he'd shown Nathan Turner and the way he'd helped her, a total stranger. "I can see that."

"So don't take offense when I ask you this, but

are you still in love with your ex? If he calls or shows up, are you going back to him?"

"No! Good lands, no. I'm not that crazy."

Cassie's shoulders relaxed. She picked up her trash bag and started walking. Annalisa joined her. "People do crazy things for love."

"Yes, they do. I have. But I won't again."

"Be careful of making that promise." Cassie bent to add a rusted pop can to her bag. "I like you, Annalisa. In such a short time, you've become a friend, like the sister I always wanted."

Annalisa swallowed the rise of emotion. The term *sister* brought visions of Olivia. "I feel the same. You and Austin and this town. Sometimes I think I'd be dead without all of you."

"Your boyfriend is a scary man."

"He was. But I can't put all the blame on him. I should have left long ago." It felt right to take responsibility for her own actions, something she hadn't done in a while. James had controlled her world, but she'd let him.

Cassie squeezed Annalisa's forearm. "Well, you're here now and God has a plan. He always had a plan for your life, but like my mule-headed brother, you weren't cooperating."

With a deep ache of longing Annalisa admitted, "I wish I knew what His plan is. Sometimes I wonder what I'm supposed to do, where to go, if I'm right or wrong."

"We all struggle with that. The best thing I can tell you is to pray, listen hard and then put one foot in front of the other. If you're going astray, God will put a check in your spirit."

That much was true. She'd felt that check before she'd gone back to James after the first time he'd hurt her. Yet, she'd ignored the tug. Now she understood that God's warning had not been to interfere in her life, but to save her from heartache. "I wish I'd listened."

"If you had, you wouldn't be here."

Interesting take on the matter, but true. Did God have a hand in that, too?

Inadvertently, Annalisa's gaze found the cowboy. His back was turned, and the muscles of his shoulders and back flexed beneath his plaid shirt as he and Davis lifted a window free from the old house. Taking care not to break the glass, they put the old window in a stack of salvageable goods.

Davis said something and Austin glanced back to catch her looking. She smiled. He lifted a gloved hand. They continued to stare across the space until Davis chucked a stick at Austin's chest and captured his attention.

What if she'd not met Austin Blackwell under Whisper Falls? What if he hadn't come to her rescue? Where would she be today?

One thing she knew for certain, she wasn't ready for a new relationship. Even though she'd grown and changed since that awful day, her judgment still needed work, and so did the rest of her life. But something sweet was fermenting between her and Austin. She thought again of God's plan. Was Austin Blackwell part of hers? Did she even want him to be?

Cassie followed the line of her gaze. With another arm squeeze, she murmured, "Don't hurt him," and moved away, leaving Annalisa to ponder.

Chapter Nine

By late afternoon the house project was well under control when Miss Evelyn had the wild idea to load up the crew of volunteers and head downtown to Easy Street.

"Pumpkins," she explained from her dais on the tailgate of a pickup truck. "Jack Macabee just called and said he had loaded a trailer with pumpkins and was heading our way. Let's go set up some displays!"

To a person, they were dirty and tired, but only a few refused to help, and those had legitimate reasons. Austin watched, wondering at the spirit of community in Whisper Falls. His hometown had been like this in many ways, but they'd turned on him when the going got tough. He couldn't help believing Whisper Falls would be the same.

"All right, crew, we'll meet at the depot in ten minutes. See you there." Miss Evelyn bustled toward her Lincoln while the rest of the group broke up and headed toward vehicles.

Cassie, Austin, Annalisa, Davis and his children and Creed Carter milled around the work site, finishing up as trucks and cars pulled away from the curb.

Austin tossed a crowbar into the back of his truck when he spotted Annalisa dragging her last filled bag of trash toward the Dumpster. He'd started toward her when she was intercepted by Creed Carter.

"I'll get that for you." The good-looking pilot took the bag, muscles flexing as he easily hefted the trash into the industrial-sized Dumpster. Dusting his hands lightly, he said, "Need a ride into town?"

Austin tensed, waiting for her answer.

Annalisa flicked a glance in his direction. "Well, I—I rode in with Austin. I guess I should go with him."

She guessed? Did she feel obligated?

He crouched to his toolbox and pretended to check the contents. He wouldn't interfere. She was a grown woman. It was probably best for everyone if she preferred the flyboy's company to his.

A truck started and then roared away.

Austin slammed the lid with more force than necessary and rose to his feet. As he expected, Creed and his truck were gone.

But then he saw Annalisa striding toward him, ponytail bopping. Her obligation comment soured his stomach.

He opened the truck door for her. "You could have ridden with Creed."

"I came with you. I didn't want to be rude."

Was that the only reason? "Who you ride with is no big deal."

She gave him a strange look before climbing with agile grace into the passenger seat. "It is to me."

Austin stewed on the comment for the next two hours while the committee of joking, chattering volunteers carted pumpkins all over the downtown area. Not that they had far to go in Whisper Falls. They'd piled the orange fruit on street corners, atop hay bales, in black kettles and brightly painted wheelbarrows.

"We don't need streetlights," Annalisa joked. "The pumpkins are bright enough to glow in the dark."

The two of them had ended up in the tiny park at midtown where someone had positioned an old wooden farm wagon. Cassie and others were working inside the gazebo while Austin and Annalisa filled the wagon with hay and pumpkins.

"I'll have nightmares," Austin said. "Attack of the killer pumpkins."

"Wasn't that a movie?"

"If it wasn't, it should be."

"But the displays are beautiful."

She was right, of course. The bright orange pumpkins, flanked by flowerpots in contrasting colors and lots of greenery, gave the streets a festive mood.

Cassie came up to them then. Her ponytail had come loose at the sides and her fingers were stained with orange. "Some of us are going to the Pizza Pan to grab a bite. Want to come?"

Austin groaned. Annalisa giggled.

"Pizza? We'll pass."

Annalisa remained quiet and just that quick, he regretted the refusal. Not that he wanted pizza, but he shouldn't have spoken for Annalisa. She'd had enough of a man telling her what to do.

"Go with them if you want to," he said to her.

She shook her head. "Maybe next time."

Her answer was the same as his, a refusal from a person tired of eating pizza. Not a desire to hang out with him. But he was glad anyway.

"You don't know what you're missing," Cassie said cheerfully as she meandered away to join the waiting group.

"What sounds good to you?" His diner sandwiches and Miss Evelyn's cookies had long since disappeared. "I'm starved."

Annalisa moved a flowerpot filled with yellow mums a couple of inches to the left of the wagon wheel. Then she placed another pot, this one filled with something purple, next to the other wheel. She fiddled with the display so long that Austin thought she either hadn't heard him or was looking for an excuse not to join him for dinner.

Finally, when he'd begun to feel dejected and stupid, she said, "I have an idea if you're game."

By now, he was getting grumpy. If she didn't want to eat with him, why hadn't she gone with Cassie? Or Creed? "What is it?"

"Let's grab a pumpkin and a carving kit and head back to the ranch."

Dubiously, he asked, "We're making pumpkin pie?"

Her laugh brought him out of his dark mood.

"Possibly, but I was actually thinking this. We can pop a casserole in the oven and while it's cooking, we'll carve a pumpkin."

"I haven't done that since I was a kid."

"Me, either. So what do you say?"

Before he could recall all the reasons he shouldn't spend an evening alone with Annalisa Keller, he said, "I say you're on."

Annalisa moved around Austin's kitchen with ease, enjoying the domestic feel of cooking for a hungry man. She was tired from the day's work, but energy sizzled through her, an adrenaline surge fueled by the pleasure of Austin's company.

She'd never expected to enjoy being with a man again after the fiasco with James, but Austin, for all his bluster, was easy to be with.

While he chopped onion, a chore that had him teary-eyed and her snickering, she sautéed chicken for a chicken and rice casserole.

"Crybaby," she said, handing him a paper towel. He took her teasing with good nature, another marvel. James wouldn't have.

Resolutely, she set her focus on slicing celery while the chicken sizzled in the skillet. James was out of the picture. She was tired of him and his fearsome temper intruding in her life, tired of comparing him to Austin. They were *nothing* alike.

"Here's the onion." He dumped the pile into the bowl with the rice and mushroom soup. "What next?"

Annalisa added the celery and chicken, stirred and spooned the mixture into a casserole dish. "Set the table and wait. The green beans are almost ready."

He gave a mock groan. "Waiting is the hard part. I'm starved."

She poked a stick of celery between his teeth. "This should hold you."

He sagged against the counter. "Men die on celery diets. We require meat."

Laughing at his silly expression, she rescued a scrap of chicken from the skillet. "Here you go."

He opened his mouth and she popped the scrap inside, her fingers brushing his lips. A shiver ran down her arms.

Austin caught her wrist and tugged. "Come here, you."

Her heart bumped. From the gleam in his green eyes, she thought for sure he was about to kiss her.

Did she want him to?

Following instinct, she moved closer.

Austin's mouth curved. "You want to know something?"

"What?" The word came out in a breathy whisper.

Austin's big cowboy rough thumb stroked her jaw. His eyes glittered and a muscle in his cheek twitched. She could sense his heart thundering as hers was, could smell the day's work and the heat of his body.

She sniffed, scenting something else, as well. "Oh, my goodness. The beans!"

With a jerk, she pulled away and rushed toward the stove and a pan of scorching green beans. Her shoulders sagged.

Austin came up behind her, took her by the upper arms and turned her around. "I've eaten worse. Cassie tried to make biscuits once."

She searched his expression, expecting something to indicate the tender emotion of a moment ago. Whatever had been about to occur was long gone, masked behind sympathy and a hint of humor over the burned beans.

"Bad biscuits?" she asked.

"Had to throw them out. Hit a bird and killed it dead."

She giggled. "Did you make that up?"

"Would I lie about a serious thing like biscuits?"

"Yes, you would."

And she liked him for it.

After dinner, Austin lined the table with newspapers and set the fattest pumpkin he could find in the center.

"Do you remember how to do this?" he asked.

"Sure." Annalisa waved a nonchalant hand. "Carving a pumpkin is like riding a horse."

Austin stared at the fat pumpkin in pretend amazement. "You put a saddle on it?"

The goofy comment made her laugh—again. She'd done a lot of that tonight and he found the sound pure magic. Every time she laughed, he looked for something else to make it happen again. A happy Annalisa was a beautiful thing.

The wondrous thought danced through him. Annalisa was happy. Maybe he was, too.

After all she'd been through, she found reasons

to smile, reasons to show kindness to others, reasons to put the past behind her and move forward determined to live life to the fullest. Unlike some people he knew. Namely him.

A man could take lessons from a woman like Annalisa.

The next morning Austin snickered to himself as Cassie and Annalisa got ready for church. Both women hobbled around the living room as if they'd been dragged behind a horse.

"I can't believe how sore my muscles are," Cassie said.

"Me, either. I thought I was in decent shape."

Annalisa looked in great shape to him, but he sipped at his second cup and said, "Pansy. I thought you were Super Trash Girl, madam pumpkin carver and bean burner extraordinaire."

She gave him a mock scowl. "Cassie, your brother is picking on me."

Cassie, hairbrush in hand, started down the hall toward the bathroom. "You're on your own, girlfriend. My back is too sore to fight with him today."

"Mine, too!" Annalisa hobbled around the bar and into the open living room where she gingerly eased into Austin's favorite TV chair. Tootsie hopped up beside her, head tilted in question. Annalisa scratched the dog's ears. "It's nothing,

Tootsie. Trash Girl will live to tote more trash and chop more weeds."

Austin watched the interaction of woman and dog. She never complained about the dog hairs on her clothes or the unmentionable substances he tracked in the back door. In fact, Annalisa didn't complain about anything.

Last night, he'd been tempted to kiss her. He was glad he hadn't, all things considered. With the two of them under the same roof, a romance could get sticky.

Their carved pumpkin resided on the kitchen table, the front half an artistic swirl of flowers, the back a horse head, the only thing he knew how to carve. They'd argued and laughed, tossed pumpkin seeds and made a mess. And he'd lain awake for hours relishing the way she'd made him feel and worrying about letting her get too close.

He poured another cup of coffee, stirred in half a spoon of creamer the way she liked it, and carried both their cups into the living room. "We have ibuprofen if you need a pain killer."

"Coffee's fine for now. Thank you." She sipped, dodging Tootsie's affectionate tongue.

"Come here, mutt." Austin took the dog from her lap. "You'll never get ready with her in the way."

Annalisa set her coffee on the squat, square end table. "Why don't you go with us this morning?"

The question caught him off guard. He blinked a few times for good measure, then scratched at his chin before saying, "I haven't been to church in a long time."

"I hadn't been, either, until recently."

So much for his strongest argument. Fact of the business, he'd been thinking about it most of the morning, thanks to her. Not about church specifically, but his relationship with God. Or lack thereof.

"Have you attended at all since moving to Whisper Falls?" She was pretty as a flower sitting in his chair in her newly purchased clothes. The peach-colored sweater buttoned over a white top and matched up real pretty with a swirly multicolored skirt. But then, he thought she'd looked great in his old shirts and Cassie's too-short jeans.

"No." He knew he was scowling and couldn't seem to stop. He'd had this conversation with himself. A relationship with God was important, but...

She tilted her head and smiled. "God's not mad at you."

"What?"

She shrugged. "I thought He was angry at me because of all the bad choices I've made."

"Yeah." He could relate. God always seemed angry to him. "Me, too."

"He's not. God loved us enough to send His Son

to die. Even when we displease Him, the only person we hurt is ourselves. God is still there, loving us and waiting for us to get a clue."

"You've been listening to my sister."

Cassie came trouncing down the hallway in skinny jeans, ruffled red shirt and high black heels. "She certainly has and you should, too. So are you coming with us or what?"

He was surprised to discover the idea appealed, but he wasn't quite ready. He'd already gotten more involved than he'd intended in the doings of Whisper Falls. Church made him vulnerable. People would ask questions. And Austin still didn't have all the answers. When he had everything figured out, maybe then.

"Davis Turner mentioned something about coming to the ranch this afternoon with his kids. I should stick around and get the horses tuned up."

"Davis attends church, Austin." Cassie slid a giant silver loop into her earlobe, her gaze holding his. "If he comes at all, it will be much later."

"We'd enjoy your company." This statement from Annalisa almost broke through his resistance. Almost.

"Why don't I hang out here and put on dinner? How about steaks on the grill?"

Cassie groaned. "You drive a hard bargain, brother, but your soul is more important."

Did she have to mention that? "Baked potatoes? Maybe some corn on the cob?"

Cassie's look was exasperated. "Will you at least think about going with us sometime soon? It won't kill you. You might actually enjoy yourself—like you did yesterday."

Cassie, of all people, knew his reasons for not allowing people into his space, and yet, she seemed intent on forcing his hand. She was right about yesterday. He'd enjoyed the day, especially getting to know Davis and Creed better. Hanging out with Annalisa last night hadn't been too bad, either.

He slid a glance toward her. She was watching him closely. Something he didn't comprehend lurked in her blue eyes.

A tug-of-war engaged in his head. He was dealing with two issues and yet they ran together like colored sand, different but intermingled. He'd lost trust in God and mankind. Annalisa had lost trust in men and herself. She was a battered woman. His battered past would not only scare her, but it could also turn her soft gaze hard with speculation and suspicion.

Sticking to the plan was safer for both of them.

That afternoon, Annalisa returned to the ranch feeling lighter and better than she had in years.

"Awesome service," she said as she and Cassie

exited the car. "About how God can take something terrible, the way he did with Joseph, and turn it into something good."

"Pastor Ed's sermons are usually relevant like that. He hits you where you live." Cassie reached back inside and took her Bible from the front seat.

The smoky aroma of grilled meat wafted across the yard. Annalisa lifted her nose to the air and sniffed. "Yum. Do you smell that?"

"My big brother has been busy."

When the car doors slammed, Jet and Hoss streaked toward the women from the direction of the barn, tails swishing. Near the same general direction, Annalisa spotted Austin moving horses into a large, fenced lot.

"He must be getting ready for Davis and his kids," Cassie said.

Annalisa watched him stroke a hand over an equine nose as he slid a halter over the massive head. The unmoving horse trusted him implicitly. A funny feeling, of yearning and hope and rightness, tingled along Annalisa's skin. She couldn't make sense of the emotions, nor could she stop watching Austin Blackwell with his horse. "He's a good man."

"Good to the soul. My brother pretends to be the big bad wolf, but he's actually the woodsman, ready to come to the rescue if anyone bothers Little Red Riding Hood."

Annalisa dragged her gaze back to Cassie. "Did he do that for you?"

"He did. When Darrell died—" Cassie paused, pursed her red, red lips while she gathered her emotions "—Austin took care of everything. Arrangements, me, Darrell. Everything. Our parents came up from Texas and wanted me to go home with them, but I couldn't. I wanted to be here where Darrell and I met and fell in love, where he's buried. Austin ran interference and convinced the folks that he needed me here on the ranch."

"He does."

Cassie laughed, but Annalisa saw the pain lurking behind the smile. "Oh, yeah. I'm such a great cook and housekeeper. And a dandy fence fixer. He couldn't get along without me."

"You're a lot more than that, and you know it." Annalisa looped arms with her friend. She felt good to have friends again, a woman to talk to, people in town who invited her places and a church to work in. The world had opened up the day James had pushed her out of his car. She'd thought it was a terrible day, but as Pastor Ed said, God had turned the situation for her good. She thanked Him daily that James was out of her life.

Cassie paused and turned back toward the barn lot. "Hey, brother, where's our steak?"

Chapter Ten

Austin rubbed his too-full belly and stretched out in the lawn chair to let the sun warm his face. A gnat swarmed his nose. He swatted lazily and squinted one eye toward Annalisa.

Since he'd cooked, she'd insisted on clearing up. Not that he planned to let her do all the work, but he did want a break.

"Be back later, guys." Cassie slammed out the back door, lipstick fresh and wallet in hand. "Sorry to leave you with the cleanup, but I promised Rusty I'd be there by two."

Mayor Fairchild had called an impromptu meeting of the Pumpkin Fest Committee. Austin grumbled to himself, wondering if Cassie was the only member.

Annalisa waved her off. "Go. Enjoy. I can get this."

"Need anything from town?"

"Not pizza," Austin muttered.

As she started off the porch, Cassie said, "You'll change your mind in a few hours."

Then she was gone and he was left alone with Annalisa. Other than last night, they'd not had much time alone here at the ranch since she'd taken the job at the Iron Horse. He'd figured that was for the best, considering the way he couldn't get her out of his head and the idiotic zing of energy he got whenever he looked at her.

Still, today was good. He liked talking to her, watching her in his house, with his dogs. Maybe later they'd walk down to the pond and toss in a hook.

"You like to fish?" he mumbled, hands clasped over his chest, eyes barely slits. A snooze wouldn't be too bad right now.

"I used to. Grandpa took us." Plates clinked as she stacked them together. "I don't like to clean them, though."

"Who does?"

"I guess that's true." She balanced their water glasses on top of the plates and added the silverware.

"Leave the rest. I'll do it."

Ignoring him, she carried the dishes inside. The kitchen sounds of dishes and refrigerator and cabinets drifted out onto the porch. The afternoon was warm and pleasant and if that wretched gnat would buzz off… He drifted, relaxed and full and more content than he'd felt in a long time.

Inside the house, the telephone began to ring. Austin struggled up from the near sleep. The back door opened and Annalisa stuck her head out. "Want me to get it?"

"Sure." The word came out garbled and slurred. She snickered and shut the door.

Austin forced himself to sit up and shake out the cobwebs. The caller was probably Davis, ready to bring Nathan and Paige for their first rides. Better get moving.

He shoved out of the lawn chair, grabbed the steak sauce and butter from the patio table and headed into the house. Cleaning the grill could wait.

As he set the condiments on the kitchen counter, he heard Annalisa's soft murmur from the living room. He wiped his hands on a dish towel and threaded the soft cloth through the oven handle, waiting for her to call him to the phone.

"Please, don't." Annalisa's pleading tone raised the hairs on the back of his neck. Realization struck like a sledgehammer to the skull. James. That could only be James.

Knocking over a chair in his haste, Austin rushed into the living room. Annalisa was perched on the edge of the couch, receiver against her ear, face whiter than Davis Turner's teeth. At his entrance, she lifted anxious eyes to his.

His heart slammed against his rib cage. This was his fault. He should never have let her answer the phone.

"Who is it? James?" he demanded, reaching for the receiver. Nodding, she drew away. The action cut him to the bone. Did she want to talk to the creep? Had James convinced her to return to California?

"Please, James," she begged. "Just leave me alone. I'm sorry—"

The fear of losing Annalisa was almost as great as the fear of James hurting her again. Austin's temper flared. He yanked the phone from her fingers and growled into the mouthpiece. "Don't ever call this number again."

Then he slammed the phone onto the cradle. "Are you all right?"

She stood, trembling. Tootsie hopped from the couch and stood by her, worried and still.

"No."

He knew it. Without considering all the reasons he shouldn't, Austin pulled Annalisa against his chest, wrapped one arm around her shoulders and cradled her head with the other. She came willingly to rest her cheek against his thundering heart. Her hair was silk and her scent was roses. She felt soft and small in his arms.

"He wants you back." He nearly choked on the statement.

"Yes."

Austin's heart plummeted. "Do you want to go back to him?"

"No!" She pushed against his shirtfront and lifted her face. Tears shimmered on the lids. "Never."

Relief slammed through him, stunning in intensity. "What did he say?"

She shook her head, golden hair swishing across his chin. A pulse beat in her throat and he fought the urge to touch it, kiss it. Kiss her and promise everything would be all right.

Austin clenched his back teeth. This wasn't about him. Nor was it about his ridiculous male need to kiss a beautiful woman. It was about protecting Annalisa.

He captured her lowered chin and raised it. "Talk to me."

She swallowed, nodded. "He knows where I am. He said—" She blew out a breath and turned her head slightly to the side.

Austin brought her attention back to him. Her irises shimmered with unshed tears. The fear he saw in the blue depths started war tom-toms pounding in his brain. Even though he wanted to growl and snarl, he kept his tone gentle. "What did he say?"

"He said I'd be sorry. That no woman was going to make a fool of him and get away with it." She started to tremble again.

"You believe him?"

Her face was grim. "James doesn't make empty threats."

"What do you suppose he means to do?"

"With James you never know. That's what makes him so scary."

"Do you think he'll come here to Whisper Falls?"

He could see she hadn't had time to think the situation through because his question brought a fresh glimmer of tears. "I pray he won't, but—"

"He very well could."

"Yes." The pulse beating in her throat pounded faster. She was terrified of the jerk.

Austin's jaw tensed as he stared at her sweet, kind face and made a vow. "If he comes here, he won't like the reception. Trust me on this, Annalisa. I will not let him hurt you again."

She touched his cheek with shaky fingers, the feel of which shook him to the soles of his boots. "You don't know James. Maybe I should leave, move on, go somewhere else. You don't deserve to be dragged into my problems."

Austin's gut clenched. The thought of letting her go cut like a surgeon's knife. "The only way I'm letting you run is if you want to leave. Do you?"

"No. No. I told you."

Austin shivered as her fingers stroked his cheek in a touch he could only describe as affectionate. Did she feel this same warm, wonderful, terrifying tenderness?

"Then you'll stay. You can't run from a bully."

"I don't want to cause problems for you and Cassie."

"You let us worry about that. We'll figure out something." He smiled, although the effort was wobbly. Holding her this close, with her face full of hope and fear had a bizarre effect on him. "Come on now," he encouraged. "Where's my Super Trash Girl? The one who says God has a plan, that He works everything for our good?"

He had a hard time believing the verses, but as he spoke, hope buoyed up that they were true.

Lips quivering, Annalisa tried to smile. With a tiny nod, she stepped back, breaking contact. Austin's heart sank. He wanted her in his arms, against his chest, the smell of her hair and perfume strong in his nose.

To keep her safe. To protect her. That was his responsibility as a man. He wanted her close enough to protect.

"I should have known he'd call again." He clenched his fist, angry that he hadn't seen this coming.

Annalisa stilled. "Again? What are you saying? Has James called here before?"

Austin raked an unsteady hand down his face. "Yeah, I think so."

She came at him, betrayal and shock in her expression. "Why didn't you tell me? How could you keep that from me?"

"The caller didn't give his name. I wasn't positive he was James."

"But it *was* him. He knows where I am, and he has for a while. You should have told me." She wrapped her arms around her chest, staring toward the window and the vast wilderness around the ranch. "He could have walked right in without warning, and I wouldn't have been on guard."

Every muscle tense enough to snap, Austin blurted, "I would have been."

Her mouth opened and closed as his words sank in. Awareness dawned. "That's why you came to the Iron Horse every day, and why you insisted on driving me everywhere, isn't it? And all this time, I thought—" She shook her head and left the sentence unfinished.

Austin knew what she'd thought. Like Miss Evelyn and Uncle Digger, and even Cassie, she'd thought he was falling for her. Resisting the urge to take her in his arms again, he knew she'd been correct, a situation as dangerous for him as James was for her.

"Would you consider taking out a restraining order?"

Her lips curled bitterly. "I've tried that trick. A cop walks right through them, undeterred. He lies about me, and his buddies cover for him."

Austin's heart stopped in his chest. "Cop?"

She must have heard the stunned tone. She tilted her head and looked at him with curiosity. "I thought I'd told you. James is a police captain. I worked for him."

Austin's head roared with the information. He fought to clear the noise and think straight. A cop. Her ex was a cop.

The roar in his head became the strobing lights of a cruiser and the wail of sirens.

Annalisa wasn't the only one tempted to run.

If a cop came calling, what on earth would he do?

Chapter Eleven

"I hate this. I hate it!" Annalisa squeezed her fists into balls. Ever since the phone call from James, she'd been looking over her shoulder constantly. Every noise made her jump.

Whenever she was alone in the snack shop, she braced herself for war each time the door opened, and then let out a shaky breath when one of the townspeople ambled in. Uncle Digger had noticed and asked what was wrong. She'd said nothing and didn't intend to. These sweet old people who'd given her a job didn't deserve the worry. James wanted to punish her, no one else.

The only thing that made her day better was when Austin arrived. Faithful as the morning, he'd mosey in and take up residence on one of the bar stools, sometimes two or three times a day.

She knew he had work to do and was neglecting the ranch for her sake. As guilty as that made her feel, she couldn't ask him to stay home. Not yet. Not while James's phone call still echoed in her mind.

This particular day, Uncle Digger was in the museum polishing Betsy, as he'd named the engine, and Miss Evelyn had bustled off to make last-minute preparations for this weekend's Pumpkin Fest. Six customers scattered over the small shop with their snacks, but even their presence didn't settle her nerves.

The door opened and she tensed, relaxing when Austin entered. He crossed to a table and spoke briefly to another rancher—Kale someone. She was still learning names. Then he nodded toward the other customers and came to the bar.

Suddenly, her world felt safe and right. "Hey, cowboy."

He removed his white hat and placed it on a stool. "Hi."

She leaned her elbows on the counter. "Coffee? Tea?"

He shook his head. "Can't stay long. I have a sick cow. Just ran in to pick up some medicine from the vet."

Hiding her disappointment, she said, "Will she be okay?"

"Should be." He reached inside his jacket and took out a box. "Bought you something."

A tingle of pleasure shot up her arms. He'd

bought her a gift? Curious, she reached for the small white box and opened the flap.

"A cell phone? I can't accept this. It's too much."

"You need one. Don't argue. I want to be able to call you and know you can call me if necessary."

She didn't know whether to laugh or cry. For a moment, she'd thought the gift meant something other than securing her safety. She'd thought— well, it didn't matter what she'd thought. She'd been wrong.

She removed the phone from the package, taking note of the touch screen and numerous apps. "But this is expensive, a fancy smartphone. You don't own one of these yourself."

"Don't want one."

"Are you always this stubborn?"

"Always. So accept the phone and stop arguing. It gives me peace of mind."

Having a cell phone would do the same for her, but she wasn't quite ready to capitulate. "You could have gone basic."

He shrugged. "You deserve the best."

Her heart lifted. Austin Blackwell had a way about him. "So do you."

A tiny grin played at the corner of his mouth. He stared at her for a few seconds before saying, "I'm working on it."

She had no idea what he meant by that.

He jabbed a finger at the new telephone. "My

number is on speed dial and also programmed by voice. Say my name and you got me."

She was tempted to say his name. "Cool."

"You might want to program in Cassie and Police Chief Farnsworth just in case."

Just in case James came calling. Just in case the sweet peace and happiness she'd found in Whisper Falls fell apart. Just in case her cowboy wasn't around when she called.

Her cowboy. The thought lingered. Was she crazy to want another man after what James had done?

Crazy or not, she thought about Austin Blackwell a lot. Beneath his terse demeanor, he was tender and thoughtful and caring. The cell phone was just one example, and in the few weeks she'd known him, she'd seen plenty more. The handsome cowboy would probably run like a racehorse if he had an inkling that his houseguest had feelings for him.

But he didn't know, and she planned to keep her feelings to herself. She could be wrong about Austin Blackwell just as she'd been about James. In the matter of men, she no longer trusted her own judgment.

Uncle Digger appeared from inside the museum as a young woman with five small children entered the Iron Horse. Annalisa recognized the auburn-haired woman as Haley Blanchard from church. Even though she didn't patronize the snack shop often, Haley always brought an entourage of children. From Cassie, she'd learned that the children were in foster care, a fact that made Annalisa's heart ache.

"Hi, Haley."

The young red-haired woman looked up in surprise. "Oh, hi. Annalisa, isn't it?"

"Yes, we met at church. What can I get for you and the children?"

"I think the consensus, as unhealthy as it may be, is corn dogs and soda. We're celebrating Thomas's win in the third-grade spelling bee."

"Congratulations, Thomas."

A little boy with big glasses and a cowlick grinned and ducked his head.

By this time, Uncle Digger had turtled his way to the newcomers. "Corndogs are on the house, Annalisa. This boy's a credit to Whisper Falls. Why, we're in the company of a champion!" To the boy, he demanded, "Spell *corn dog.*"

Thomas sat up straight as an arrow. "Corn dog. *C-o-r-n d-o-g.* Corn dog."

"See what I mean?" Uncle Digger marveled. "A champion indeed. Corn dogs on the house!"

The five children giggled and lit up like a small unmatched set of Christmas lights. Uncle Digger patted Thomas on the shoulder. "I got free train tickets, too. For you and—" he looked over the group gathered around the table "—five others. Why, look here, Thomas. Just the right amount for all of you to take a ride on my train."

"Corn dogs coming up." Feeling warm and fuzzy from Uncle Digger's generous offer, Annalisa went to get the order. As she passed Austin, who had turned to watch the children, he handed her the phone she'd left on the counter.

"Keep this in your pocket."

"Will do, boss." She slid the sleek new device into her apron. "Thank you. And don't worry."

"I'd feel better if you'd let me apprise Chief Farnsworth."

Her fear that James's influence was as far-reaching as the Whisper Falls Police Department might be irrational, but it was real. "Things are better this way."

He sighed. "Still planning to attend Pumpkin Fest on Saturday?"

Her pulse kicked up. "Yes."

"Alone?"

"Not sure yet. Maybe with friends from church. A few of the singles have been talking about hanging out together."

"Oh." He nodded, slid off the stool. "Okay."

"Why?"

He took up his hat and crimped the edges with strong fingertips. "I don't like the idea of you going alone."

Then go with me, you dolt. "Neither do I."

"But if you're in a group, I guess you'll be all right."

"I'll be fine."

"All right, then. I guess that settles it." And he shoved the hat onto his head and walked out.

Austin wasn't happy about Annalisa going off to the Pumpkin Fest without a single one of her friends knowing she could be in danger. He read the papers. He'd heard of men who, out of spite and rage, chased down their exes, hauled them into a dark corner and murdered them.

He shuddered at the macabre thought. Death was a companion with which he was far too well acquainted. He was not going to let James Winchell get close to Annalisa, even if he had to follow her around the busy festival the way Jet and Hoss followed him around the ranch.

"You're certainly in a snit," Cassie said as she tossed a plastic grocery bag onto the table next to her purse and cell phone.

"I hope you didn't bring pizza," he grumbled.

She jacked a snarky eyebrow at him. "You're in luck, grouchy. Annalisa wants to cook. Why else would I tote in grocery bags?"

He closed the three-ring binder filled with his cattle records and shoved the ledger to one side. "Where is she?"

"Ah, so that's the problem. Your sweetie is out of your line of vision and that makes you cranky."

"She's not my sweetie."

"Whatever you say." She thumped a package of chicken breasts onto the counter with a little more force than necessary.

He ambled to the grocery bags and took a peek. "Well?"

"Well, what?"

"Where is she? She's supposed to ride home with you. You're supposed to keep an eye on her."

With mild reproof, she said, "She's a big girl, Austin. She doesn't need us to keep an eye on her."

Austin didn't agree, but he kept his mouth shut.

"Miss Evelyn will drive her home later. They had some things to do in the snack shop in preparation for Pumpkin Fest."

"She's working tomorrow?" He'd never considered that, but he liked the idea. She'd be in an easily contained space, and he could hang out at the Iron Horse without appearing too obvious. Looking out for her at the crowded festival was a problem—unless he was with her.

He didn't want people getting ideas about that, either. Especially his sister who seemed determined to create a romance between him and Annalisa. Regardless of how he felt, love was a risk neither he nor Annalisa could take. And with

Annalisa's ex-boyfriend being a cop, Austin's big fat can of worms could spring open at any given moment. A real romance killer right there, if ever there was one. To keep his shame firmly in the past, he had to keep his attraction to Annalisa under wraps.

"Just for a couple of hours," Cassie said. "She's working through lunch while Miss Evelyn runs the parade and Uncle Digger gives train rides."

Oh. So much for plan A.

"She still should have let me know she was staying late."

Cassie struck a pose, hand on hip. "Brother, dear, for a man who claims not to be smitten, you certainly are possessive."

"I have my reasons. You know what Annalisa was like when she first arrived. Battered, scared, bruised."

"I know. I know," she said softly. "Interesting how you didn't want her here back then. Now you can't bear to have her out of your sight."

"You know why."

"I'm beginning to think so."

"Don't go there," he warned. Then to avoid more of Cassie's troublesome line of conversation, Austin reached into a grocery bag and pulled out ground beef, mushrooms, peppers, onions and cheddar cheese. The menu was getting interesting. "What is she making?"

"Don't know. I shop. She cooks."

"And I eat." He shoved the perishables inside the fridge and withdrew a pitcher of ice water.

Cassie's red lips twisted into a smile. "Getting rather domesticated around here, aren't we?"

"Nothing wrong with that."

"And it's all because of Annalisa." She extended a drinking glass. Austin filled the tumbler, mulling on her comment as Cassie added, "She's awesome."

"Yeah." *Awesome* was the word. Annalisa was easygoing and honest and hardworking, not at all the kind of person he'd judged her to be at first. If she'd lied, she'd done so out of fear, not because she was dishonest. His blood still boiled every time he thought about James's abuse and the broken arm.

As if she'd read his thoughts, Cassie asked, "Do you really think her boyfriend will come after her?"

"Ex-boyfriend, and I hope not."

"What if he does?"

"I don't know." He'd wondered the same thing many times. Mostly, he'd like to beat the cretin to a bloody pulp. Now that he knew James was a cop, though, he wasn't sure what he would do.

"I've been praying about the situation," Cassie said, "praying for her safety, praying for her to have wisdom."

In the past, religious talk had made him uncomfortable. Not so much today. Not that he thought it would do any good, but if prayer would protect Annalisa, he was ready to pull an all-nighter.

"I've been praying about something else, too, Austin." Cassie leaned a hip on the edge of the counter. "You should tell her about Blair."

He clumped his drinking glass onto the table. "No."

"Why not? You can trust Annalisa. She's not going to bolt at the first sign that your life hasn't been perfect."

But he feared she might. "I don't want her to know. There's no point in her knowing."

Cassie slid away from the counter and came to him. "Are you sure about that, big brother? Are you sure there's no reason to open your heart? Are you sure there's not something really special happening between the two of you?"

He stared into green eyes so like his own and saw the reflection of a man who'd come to a crossroads. And he didn't know which road to take.

The morning of Pumpkin Fest dawned cloudy and cool with a definite autumn snap in the air. Austin shrugged into a warm jacket as he headed out to the barn to feed the horses and check on his sick cow. When he returned, Cassie had already gone into town to help align the floats for the parade. Annalisa had breakfast on the table, a fact that made him feel guilty. Cassie's words had haunted him all night, enough to give a man indigestion.

"You don't have to cook for me, Annalisa. I've told you that before."

She looked sunny and bright in her pumpkin T-shirt and blue jeans, the results of a shopping trip with his sister. "I like to cook. It makes me feel worthwhile. That is, if you don't mind."

"Mind? I could eat your food all day and never get tired of it."

The compliment brightened her face. "Good. Then, sit down and eat and don't make a fuss."

He did. And while he chewed fried sausage and fluffy, syrup-laden pancakes, he chewed on the Pumpkin Fest situation, too. The more he thought about it, the more he didn't like the idea of Annalisa alone at the festival with people who didn't know she could be in danger. In such a large gathering, no one would ever notice one more stranger. The fest was the perfect place for James to make good on his threat.

"I'm going to the festival," he said.

"But you said you never go."

"First time for everything."

Annalisa slid into a chair across from him. Her plate, contrary to his, contained only one pancake topped with blueberries. She poked a fork tine into one blueberry. "Everyone says they have a great time. I've been looking forward to today."

"So I was thinking," he went on as if she hadn't commented, "maybe we should go together. Just to be on the safe side."

He held his breath, expecting her to refuse. After all, she already had plans with friends.

She studied him for one beat and then said, "Okay."

Surprised, Austin rested his fork atop his syrup-saturated pancake while his gaze met hers. She smiled. An answering grin spread across his face. Warmth came with it, a warmth that invaded his chest and curled right around his heart.

"Well," he said, "all right, then." He jabbed a bit of pancake. "All right."

Police Chief JoEtta Farnsworth sailed up and down Easy Street on her scooter, siren wailing as she cleared the parade route. Annalisa thought the stocky fiftysomething chief was a comical sight in her Amelia Earhart helmet and goggles and shiny black leather pants, but she handled the town's security without a flinch.

Annalisa had seriously considered telling the chief about James, but a part of her didn't want to believe he'd follow through with his threats. Another part of her wondered if James might have discovered her whereabouts through the police chief. It wouldn't be the first time he'd used his contacts and charm to gain information. But California was far, far away. Surely he wouldn't come so far because of anger and revenge.

As far as the eye could see, pumpkins lined every empty spot up and down the main drag of Whisper Falls. Displays by schoolchildren and art groups, churches and businesses perched on tables and makeshift benches created from a board and concrete blocks. A pumpkin tower, at least three stories high, rose next to the train station. The valleys and farms around Whisper Falls produced a lot of pumpkin!

She chanced a look at Austin. He'd been clear that their "date" was nothing more than guard duty, but she was happy to be with him anyway. As he walked alongside her down the narrow sidewalk, she felt safe and…connected.

"Listen to that," she said.

A montage of music filled the air—bluegrass, gospel, country—along with the redolent smells of vendors firing up their specialties. Everything from turkey legs to funnel cakes mingled with the overriding fragrance of pumpkin. Local cooks had outdone themselves to create a variety of pumpkin-flavored recipes. Pumpkin candy, pies, casseroles, even pumpkin lasagna.

"I have to try pumpkin candy at some point," she said, intrigued that such a thing existed.

"It's actually good."

"You've had it?"

"Pumpkin praline fudge. Cassie forced it on me once. Instant fan." He patted his flat belly. "I'll buy you some at Sweets and Eats. Edie makes the best in town."

Annalisa arched a teasing eyebrow. "You're a pumpkin candy connoisseur?"

"Shucks, no, ma'am," he teased in return. "I'm just a lowly cowpoke whose sister feeds him nothing but junk food. The fudge was her idea of supper."

With a chortle, she pushed at his shoulder. He caught her fingers. "That hand is getting out of control. I'd better hold on to it for you."

His was the smoothest method of holding a girl's hand that she'd ever witnessed. And Annalisa hadn't a single objection. As Austin wrapped his fingers around hers and pulled her away from the crowd, happiness bubbled inside.

They found an open place from which to view the parade, although more people crowded in every second. Cassie had warned her that the population swelled into the thousands during Pumpkin Fest. Annalisa found herself searching the faces f or a burly man with golden hair. As much as she wanted to forget the danger, James was never far from her thoughts. The cowboy at her side was a strength she was coming to depend on, but she doubted even he was a match for James's devious schemes.

They were swathed in an ocean of people gathered outside the diner when someone called her name. Her body jerked.

Austin tugged her closer. "You okay?"

She nodded, feeling foolish as she waved to Davis Turner and his children coming in their direction. Apparently, little Nathan had spotted them first. He hopped up and down, waving and calling their names.

"Look, Dad, it's Austin." Nathan shook loose from his dad's hand. "Austin, Austin."

Austin released his hold on Annalisa. Instantly, she missed him.

"How ya doin', Nathan? Ready for another ride?" Austin offered a fist bump which the boy eagerly returned.

"I sure am. When can I come?"

"Not so fast, Nathan," Davis said, shaking hands with Austin. "Sorry about that. He gets carried away at the mention of a horse."

"No problem. I invited him." Austin crouched down to eye level with the boy. "Anytime your dad can bring you, you're welcome."

Nathan's face glowed with happiness. "All right! How is Tinker? Can I ride him again?"

The affable old gelding had a lot of miles on him and was the perfect horse for a beginner.

"I think old Tinker's been missing you."

"He has?" Fists raised, Nathan waved his arms up and down. "Did you hear that, Dad? Tinker misses me."

Annalisa witnessed the conversation, her heart swelling with tenderness, both for the boy and the cowboy who'd made the child's day. Austin Blackwell was an easy man to love.

The notion brought her up short and formed a knot in her stomach. Given her track record and the threat of James coming to call, falling in love should be the last thing on her mind. It should be, but it wasn't.

Troubled by the dilemma, she turned away from the conversation to watch a clown in a tiny car spin in circles.

After a second or two, she shut her eyes against the sight. But like the clown, her head spun and the kaleidoscope world seemed out of control.

Chapter Twelve

She was nervous. Austin had felt the tension through their entwined fingers.

He watched the thirty-minute parade with half-hearted interest, his main focus the crowd of faces, many of whom he didn't recognize. If James was present, how would he know? He'd never even seen a photo of the creep.

All he could do was remain alert and ready.

The high school cheerleaders came by, chanting for the Whisper Falls Warriors. Last year, the high school team had gone to the state play-offs, although they'd not won. A football fanatic, Austin was tempted to check out a few games. He hadn't, but he'd thought about it. He missed the noise and smell and excitement of high school football.

Perched on the bed of a bright blue pickup with crepe paper streamers flying from the windows, the perky cheerleaders tossed candy and gum into the crowd. Kids scrambled toward the goodies like startled mice.

"Aren't you going to jockey for some candy?" Annalisa teased.

"I think I could take on those little guys," he joked in return. "But look at Bubba out there. That kid would take out my knees for a Tootsie Roll pop."

Annalisa laughed as the candy-tossing cheerleaders moved onward, pressed into action by the *rat-a-tat* of an advancing snare drum and a high-stepping majorette. Behind the band's rousing "I Feel Good," a handful of homemade floats from churches, clubs and the Girl Scouts rumbled past. Last of all, trotted the Round-Up Clubs in rows of four abreast, the horses decked out in fancy breast harnesses and bright saddle blankets."

"Why don't you belong to that?" Annalisa asked, taking note of the prancing color guard.

"Never thought about it." Which wasn't exactly true. What he meant was he didn't want to share his reasons. "What time do you head over to the Iron Horse?"

As the last of the horses clopped by, the parade ended and people began crossing the littered street. Excited kids scoured for unclaimed candy. Elbows and shoulders jostled against him.

Annalisa glanced at the clock on the new cell phone. "Soon. The time is close to eleven now."

Cassie had teased him about the expensive device. He didn't care. He'd wanted Annalisa to have it.

"Let's walk that direction. We can sample the booths and look at the exhibits along the way."

"Isn't there something you'd rather do than babysit me?"

"Not a thing."

"You have to get bored sitting around a snack shop while I dole out nachos and sodas."

"I eat. That's not boring." As long as Annalisa was in the shop, he wasn't bored in the least.

She bumped him with her shoulder. "You know what I mean. If there are any particular exhibits you want to see, you can do that while I'm working."

There were a few events that had caught his attention—chain saw carving, a hawg calling contest and the antique car show—but none were as important as her safety.

"Not happening, Annalisa." His tone turned serious. "Not with this many people in town."

She caught her bottom lip between her teeth. "You're worried."

"Aren't you?"

"All the time."

The reply twisted in his gut. No one should have to live with that kind of stress. But however he sliced the situation, he was anxious, too. An abusive ex-boyfriend who was also a cop could hurt them both.

He squeezed her fingers. "I'm hanging with you. Afterward, we'll get our sugar rush at Sweets and Eats and then use up all that energy at the carnival. What do you say? Ferris wheel or roller coaster?"

"Roller coaster, definitely."

"Ah, a daredevil. Roller coaster, it is. I just hope you aren't disappointed."

"Why would I be?"

"You haven't seen the Whisper Falls carnival. But if you're nice, I'll use my famous fast ball to win you a teddy bear at the baseball throw."

"I didn't know you played baseball."

There were a lot of things she didn't know about him, some that mattered, most didn't.

They strolled past a display of gourd art, everything from birdhouses to planters to lampstands. Annalisa paused and smoothed her fingers over a beautifully painted gourd vase.

Austin flipped the container upside down to read the price. Not bad if she liked it.

"I played a little ball in high school," he said. "Baseball, football. You can't be a male in Texas unless you like football."

"I've heard that." She lifted a bowl carved with colorful leaves, read the price and returned it. "Was Cassie a cheerleader? She's the perky type."

"She was. Mom and Dad followed us around half of Texas to watch. Like most parents, Dad thought I was good enough to play college. I wasn't. I preferred working on the ranch anyway."

They moved away from the gourd art to continue their trek down Easy Street, dodging humanity along the way.

"Cassie told me your parents are still in Texas, on the family ranch."

"That's right."

Out in the center of the street, a clogging troupe danced into action to the beat of "Rocky Top."

"You miss them?" Annalisa asked above the music.

"We drive down to see them pretty often. Never miss a holiday." As much as he dreaded returning to his hometown, going home to the family ranch was the right thing to do. His parents weren't getting any younger and the tragedies in the lives of their children had taken a toll. "Sometimes I feel guilty for leaving them alone."

"I know what you mean. Once they're gone from your lives—" She left the sentence dangling, but he understood where she was headed.

"Family's a good thing," he said. "It must be tough being alone in the world." Really tough, considering the company she'd been keeping.

"Not all families are happy."

True enough, even though his expectations had

been high when he'd married Blair. He should have listened to his dad.

"Cassie and I were fortunate. Good parents, strong family values." In his years of anger, he'd put aside the faith of his family. Suddenly, awareness swamped him. His good upbringing had been founded on the solid foundation of Christ. "Christian values."

"I didn't have that. I came to Jesus when a friend invited me to church. I'd never really gone to church until then."

He couldn't imagine. From the moment of memory, he'd been to church every Sunday. He'd fallen asleep under the pews, colored in Jesus coloring books, grown up in the bosom of a strong congregation.

"Your grandparents didn't attend?"

"No. Grandpa was a Christian, but he had issues with his church. I never asked what happened. He stopped going long before I was born."

"His values must have rubbed off," he said, though her revelation explained some things about the choices she'd made.

"I hope so."

They crossed the street, treading on an old brick pathway. On the corner, a dummy built of pumpkins and colorful gourds pointed toward the train station, a sign in his "hand" proclaiming all-day train rides and plenty of Miss Evelyn's almost-famous pie.

"Is that some of Miss Evelyn's handiwork?" he asked.

"Mine and hers. We worked on it last night." She tugged his hand, hurrying him up the steps of the depot. "Wait until you see the inside decorations."

At that moment, the train whistle blew, a blast that had them both flinching. With a *chug-chug* and a puff of smoke, Betsy the engine and Uncle Digger hauled slowly out of the depot loaded to the top with sun-kissed passengers.

When the noise subsided, Annalisa said, "Uncle Digger and Miss Evelyn are taking the train out tomorrow after church. They invited me to go along. Want to come?"

"He doesn't run the train on Sunday."

"It's not an actual run. Miss Evelyn wants to snap new photos for the website while the foliage is ablaze."

Austin shook his head. "Miss Evelyn and her website. She's turned this town on its ear."

"So I've heard. She's also packing a picnic lunch. It's a chance for me to see more of the famous Ozarks."

She *had* been tied down since her arrival. No car, a broken arm and friends who never took her anywhere except work and church. Some friend.

The *chop-chop-chop* of a helicopter sounded overhead. They both glanced up as Creed flew above the trees and highlines, tourists on board.

"Sure you wouldn't rather go up in Creed's chopper?"

Her answer was a smile. "Evelyn says the view from the train is stunning this time of year."

Probably even better from the chopper, but he didn't say so. "I usually prefer a real horse to an iron one, but the Ozarks *are* pretty spectacular in the fall—a sight not to be missed."

"Good. You'll go, then. Can I talk you into church, as well?"

He pretended to frown. "You're pushing your luck, lady."

She made a face at him. "It was worth a shot."

Hadn't he just been thinking about the role faith had played in his upbringing? "I might surprise you one of these days."

She smiled softly as she reached for the snack shop door. "Ready when you are."

"I coulda won the big one." Austin rotated his right arm like a windmill.

"You could have wasted another thirty dollars, too." Annalisa was amused at the big cowboy's chagrin. He'd spent far too much money to win the six-inch purple-and-white teddy bear. "I like this one." She kissed it on the black pom-pom nose. "He's perfect."

The sun had set hours ago, but the lively, noisy carnival was bright as day. She was charmed, not disappointed, although the carnival was a pitiful thing in comparison to an amusement park. Of the dozen or so rides, less than half were thrill rides and only the Zipper had made her scream. Her feet ached and she was exhausted, but she'd had more fun today than in a long time. Years, if she told the truth.

"You're only saying that to make me feel less of a failure."

Playfully, she whacked him with the teddy bear.

"Hey, that's my throwing arm." He rubbed the spot and frowned, but she knew he joked. He had been in fine form this afternoon. Maybe because there had been no sign of James, they'd both relaxed as the day wore on. He hadn't forgotten, she was certain by the way he never let her out of his sight, but they didn't talk about the threat.

Around them barkers hollered to attract customers, ride sirens screamed louder than the riders and the constant roar of generator motors kept up the steady glow of brightly colored lights and fueled the rides.

"Want to ride anything else?" she asked.

"I've been spun and whirled enough tonight to be a milk shake. I'm done."

"Me, too," she said, tugging on his elbow. "Let's get some cotton candy to munch on during the fireworks display."

"Sweet!" he said.

They both laughed at the intentional pun, and happiness spiraled up into Annalisa throat with the power of a Tilt-a-Whirl. In some ways, Austin reminded her of Grandpa Sims, the only decent male in her life. A man as strong as the land he ranched, steady and dependable, a good soul. Why had she ever been attracted to an egomaniac whose idea of manliness was a gym workout, bulky muscles and pushing others around?

"Boy or girl?"

"What?" When she saw him pointing at the blue-and-pink cotton candy, she understood. "Boy."

But the image of babies swathed in blues and pinks danced around in her head. Had Austin and his wife wanted children?

"I figured you for the pink type," he said. "Girly-girly."

"A woman doesn't want to be too predictable."

"Well, *I'm* not getting pink." He looked at the fluffy sugar with a horror that made her smile.

"Why did I know that?"

He held up two fingers to the vendor. "Two bags of blue cotton candy."

Annalisa opened her wallet, but he pushed her hand away. "My treat."

"But you've paid for everything," she protested.

He shrugged her off. "Call me old-fashioned. A man pays for the date."

Oh. Annalisa went silent. He considered this bizarre situation a date rather than guard duty?

As they walked away, each toting a blue bag of spun sugar, she gathered her nerve. "Is this a date?"

He didn't look at her. Instead, he kept a steady pace, hand on her elbow as they moved through the crowd gathering for the fireworks. "Do you want it to be?"

"I'm not sure. Do you?"

This time he stopped to look at her. She could see the wheels turning, the indecision. She understood because she felt the same. When he finally spoke, he didn't help at all. "Let's leave well enough alone, okay?"

What else could she say but "Okay."

Austin stewed on Annalisa's question the entire three blocks to the city park. Was this a date? Did he want it to be?

All right, so he did. Now what?

As they crossed the park in search of a good place to view the fireworks, a spectacle he'd never bothered to witness in Whisper Falls, they bumped into Cassie with the mayor. He didn't know why, but the idea of his sister with the boyish mayor bugged him.

"Austin, Annalisa!" With an irritating enthusiasm, Cassie tugged Rusty Fairchild toward them. "Rusty, you know my brother, and this is Annalisa from the snack shop."

Rusty offered a freckled grin. "Of course, I've met Annalisa, the pretty new seller of Miss Evelyn's famous pie."

"Almost famous," Annalisa corrected with a smile.

"What do you think of your first Whisper Falls Pumpkin Fest?"

"Wonderful so far."

"Heading for the fireworks?"

"We are."

"We'd ask you to join us, but Cassie's in charge of the music and I'm off to make sure the volunteer fire fighters showed up for duty. Can't have pyrotechnics without someone to put out the fire!"

Rusty's comment was a relief to Austin. For a minute there he'd thought the mayor would invite them to sit together. And he didn't want to do that. His sister's speculative glances were already getting under his skin. Besides, the date question still revolved in his brain with the same dizzying speed as something called the Zipper, a carnival attraction that had turned him every way but loose.

The wild ride consisted of individual metal cars made for two people. Nice that it turned out that way, now that he thought about it. Each unit was attached to an arm that spun. The car also tumbled and twisted, an action that made remaining in one spot on the inside next to impossible. He'd held on to the bar with an iron grip, but Annalisa had been thrown his direction over and over again, completely out of control, until he'd finally grabbed her and hung on for the thrill. She'd screamed so loud and laughed so hard, his ears still throbbed.

And he had loved every minute of the crazy, spinning ride with Annalisa in his arms. Him, a hardnosed cowboy who didn't even like people, had a blast at a small-town carnival with a big-time lady.

"Let's find a seat," he said after Cassie and Mayor Opie moved away.

"Where?"

Annalisa was right. The three rows of bleachers were already packed. A number of spectators had carried in lawn chairs. Austin wished he'd done the same.

"Good question."

"I don't mind standing."

She wouldn't. Annalisa didn't complain. He liked that about her. She took what came her way and made the best of the situation. Take the job at the Iron Horse, for instance. Not exactly a fancy place to work. Lousy pay. But not once had she complained that hawking snacks and train tickets was beneath her.

"We'll find a place."

The first blast of raining color had ripped the inky sky before they settled for a grassy spot next to a tree, the rough bark at their backs.

Faces lifted upward to enjoy the display, they didn't speak for a while. When they did, it was only to comment on the spectacular bursts of color. Whisper Falls made up for the puny carnival and homespun parade with a terrific pyrotechnic event.

As yet another rocket sounded, Austin angled in Annalisa's direction. Her chin was tilted upward, face illuminated by the overhead explosion of red and white. He couldn't help staring at the smooth arch of her throat and the curve of her jaw. She was a beautiful woman. Inside and out. The unnamed yearning returned, the one that had gnawed at him over and over again for days.

A snapping shower of sparks floated to the ground, crackling into silence.

Annalisa, eyes wide with enjoyment, turned and caught him staring.

Against the backdrop of a radiant exploding

sky, amid the ocean of humanity, everything faded except them.

Shadows moved across her face, framing her in dark and light. Like everyone on the planet, she was not all good and not all bad. Just a woman, a woman who made mistakes and strove to correct them. A woman who made his heart sing and yearn for better than he'd ever known. Who made him long to erase the past mistakes and start his life anew.

"Austin?" she whispered when he went on staring.

"Hmm?" His hat dipped low. His pulse hummed, hot inside his veins.

"What are you thinking?"

He considered the question a long, long time. Would she bolt if he told her the truth? Maybe. But what if...

Blame the romantic fireworks or brain fever from too many carnival rides, but he needed to know. "I'm wondering what you'd think if you knew how much I want to kiss you."

Her lips, shiny in the sparse lighting, parted. "Really?"

"What do you think? Will you slap me?"

She touched his cheek. "Only if you don't kiss me."

A Roman candle exploded. Oohs and aahs rose from the crowd. Heart pumping louder than carnival music, Austin tenderly touched his lips to hers. She tasted sweet as cotton candy, warm as summer. And the best fireworks of the night occurred behind Austin's eyelids and inside his heart.

Chapter Thirteen

Austin went to church Sunday morning. He'd risen early to care for the animals and by the time Annalisa rose, he was showered and dressed, his black hair slicked and damp, his jaw smooth and handsome.

Cassie hadn't said a word about the unexpected turn of events, so Annalisa took her cue from the sister who knew her brother best. He drove them in his pickup, a truck he'd washed and cleaned at some point since last night, even though they'd arrived home from the fireworks after midnight.

After the kiss that had rocked her world.

"What did you think of Pumpkin Fest?" Cassie asked.

She sat against the passenger door, black hair sleek and curving on the shoulders of a multicolored blouse, red lipstick vivid against white skin. Annalisa sat sandwiched in the middle, her knee bumping Austin's thigh, as they wound the curvy dirt roads leading into Whisper Falls.

"Loved it," Annalisa answered. The day had been as perfect as any she'd spent, even with the dread of seeing James again. And the ending had been even better.

"What about you, Austin?"

"Good times."

He seemed especially quiet this morning, and Annalisa understood. Or at least she thought she did. Last night's kiss lingered between them, the ignored elephant in the room. Selfishly, she wished Cassie had driven her own car so that she and Austin could talk. If he would. So far, he seemed inclined to ignore what had happened. Did he regret the impulsive act? Was he worried she'd read more into a simple kiss than he'd intended?

Somehow she didn't think so.

She'd fallen asleep last night thinking of that moment of pure bliss. The gruff, tough cowboy had been achingly tender as he'd wrapped her in a protective cocoon of sweet, sweet affection.

Her heart had leaped and danced as she'd returned the kiss. She'd burrowed close, reveling in his strength and touch.

Perhaps he'd been carried away, a result of standing beneath the glow of romantic fireworks on a perfect fall evening. Perhaps the kiss had meant nothing at all. But one thing she knew, Austin had stirred emotions that both thrilled and frightened, emotions that could leave her vulnerable yet again.

After a woman had been a fool, how did she ever get past the fear of making another poor choice?

Upon arrival at church, Annalisa shelved thoughts of last night as she greeted new acquaintances. There was a welcome here that drew her in like Sunday supper at Grandma Sims's.

Austin, too, was immediately approached by people he knew, including Davis, who was fast becoming a friend. For a man who held himself apart, a friend like Davis was a good thing.

The conversation was mostly about the successful festival, and spirits ran high. The church was far noisier than usual.

The worship leader, a guitarist, strummed the opening chords to "Open the Eyes of My Heart, Lord," and the chatter died down as people took their seats.

Austin settled in between Cassie and Annalisa, his thigh touching hers. He'd worn new jeans and a sport coat with well-polished boots, leaving his hat behind for once. His hair, now dry, was short and tidy except for the intentional muss in the front. Annalisa thought him the handsomest man in the building.

While Pastor Ed preached, Annalisa struggled to keep her mind off the cowboy and on the sermon. She should be thanking God that Austin had come to church, not thinking about kissing him.

She chanced a peek in his direction. From his focused attention on Pastor Ed, she and their kiss was the furthest thing from his mind. As it should be.

She clenched her hands together in her lap and squeezed her eyes shut to pray. Austin's face and voice and kiss intruded.

When the service ended, guilt struck. She couldn't remember much of anything the preacher had said.

As slow and powerful as an awakening giant the Whisper Falls touring train *chug-chugged* out of the little depot and into the afternoon sunshine. In his familiar striped overalls, suspenders and blue conductor's cap, Uncle Digger manned Betsy the engine. Miss Evelyn stood at his side talking a mile a minute while she waved at anyone and everyone they passed. Betsy clattered through the intersection at First and Easy before starting the uphill climb out of town.

The streets were a mess, but volunteer cleanup crews manned the job this Sunday afternoon, gathering trash left from the festival. Austin felt a little guilty at the work his sister and others were doing while he was merrily riding a train. Guilty, yes, but not enough to back out.

Balancing with his feet wide, even though the rocking train wasn't all that hard to walk in, he made his way toward the passenger car where Annalisa stood with her face pressed to the windows. Having an entire train to themselves felt odd even if there were only three cars, an engine and a caboose. Not that he was complaining. He'd probably never have ridden the train at all with the cars crowded with tourist types and nosy neighbors.

He stepped up beside Annalisa, and she turned her head slightly to smile and acknowledge his presence. His heart beat faster, a steady hum in his blood. Yesterday stayed in his head, a sweet, lively memory. Kissing her had sealed his fate. He was terrified of falling in love, especially with her, knew he couldn't allow it, had kicked himself a dozen times for kissing her. And yet, if given the chance, he'd kiss her again in a heartbeat. Not just kiss her, but hold her and look into her eyes and cherish her laugh and her goodness. For regardless of her arguments to the contrary, Annalisa Keller was a special woman.

Her breath fogged against the window pane. Miles of red-and-gold forest passed like slides on a slide show. Comfortable in her company, he said nothing, just breathed in nature's glory and Annalisa's perfume.

"Stunning, isn't it?" she said at last. "My eyes want to drink in all that beauty and hold it inside."

"God does good work." His words surprised him, an echo of something Annalisa had said weeks ago on their impromptu trail ride. He hadn't given God credit for anything good in a long time.

"He does." She turned sideways, her slender body taking up half the space his did. "Uncle Digger says we can walk out on the back of the caboose if we hold on for dear life. Want to try it?"

In the blue sweater she'd worn the first time he'd seen her, she was every bit as lovely the foliage outside the window—a bluebird amid the golds and reds. "I'm game if you are."

They made their way out on the small deck extending from the back of the little red caboose. Wind, chilled by the speed, sucked at their balance. Austin held tight to Annalisa with one hand and to the rail with the other. Her pale hair flew out in all directions. One heavy strand slapped his face. Annalisa laughed and grabbed the railing with both hands. The roar of the train filled his ears. Talking was difficult although they managed a few well-shouted comments.

"The trestle," she said, pointing at a curve ahead where a trestle spanned an enormous gulch.

Butterflies fluttered in Austin's stomach.

"Maybe we should go back inside."

"Are you kidding me?" she yelled, face aglow from wind and enjoyment. "And miss this?"

"Aren't you scared?"

"Out of my mind. That's the fun of it."

The train rounded the curve and Austin braced for the trestle, a skinny twelve-story-high track with nothing to hold the train in place but the wheels themselves. "Are you sure about this?"

Her laugh turned to a squeal as she white-knuckled the railing in front of her. Austin didn't mind heights, but twelve stories in open air was way out of his comfort zone. Heart in his mouth, he braced behind Annalisa, clasping the railing on either side as he blocked her in with his whole body. Beyond the trestle was a sheer plunge into nothingness. The chill wind whipped, the train rocked and the world clattered past in a dazzling array of color and dizzying height.

As the train gained the trestle's end and rumbled onto level ground, Annalisa loosened her death grip and turned in Austin's arms. Her hair spun around her head like gold cotton candy. "That was awesome!"

No, she was awesome, and if she didn't stop smiling up at him with her expression alive and excited, he'd be sorely tempted to kiss her again, something he shouldn't do. Keeping an eye out for her was one thing. Kissing her had jacked things to a whole different level—the danger zone.

* * *

Halfway through the twenty-mile trip, the train chugged slower and slower. Annalisa and Austin made their way through the caboose and three vintage passenger cars to the engine where Uncle Digger guided the train to a stop. The old engine coughed and hissed and let out a long sigh as the conductor shut it down.

"Perfect picnic spot," Miss Evelyn declared. "Isn't it, Digger, honey?"

"Perfect like you." He blew the train whistle once for good measure. Annalisa clapped her hands over her ears.

Miss Evelyn gave him a coy smile and a peck on the cheek, her affections obvious. Annalisa watched the older couple with a hitch beneath her ribs. She wanted a love like theirs, long and steady and comforting. A love to depend on, a love that appreciated instead of tearing down.

But Miss Evelyn and Uncle Digger were old-school, from a different era. Was their kind of relationship even possible in this modern age?

As the four of them set out the picnic lunch, Annalisa chewed on her thoughts. Occasionally, she shot a glance at Austin, wondering what he was thinking. So much had transpired between them in the short time she'd been in Whisper Falls, but she had baggage and so did Austin. He had a wife. A late wife he refused to discuss.

How terrible his grief must be.

And where did that leave her? Was she foolish to think something other than Austin's innate kindness and protectiveness blossomed between them?

"Fried chicken, tater salad, cookies and some other good things. Help yourself." Miss Evelyn opened a Tupperware container and released the smell of cold fried chicken.

With appreciative comments, they filled their plates and settled on an old quilt to eat. The meadow spreading out from the train tracks to a stand of woods wasn't large, but the glade was beautiful. Fallen leaves cluttered the fading grass in a tapestry of burgundy, orange and brown. Tiny white flowers with yellow centers surrounded the quilt. She plucked one and stuck it behind her ear.

"Pretty," Miss Evelyn said. "Don't you think so, Digger, honey?"

He plucked one of the flowers and handed it to his wife, whose ever-rosy cheeks deepened in color. "A flower for a fair maiden."

"Silly man," she blustered, but Annalisa could tell she was pleased. "I think I'll take a walk in the woods. Work off some of this dinner and take a few photos. Anyone care to join me?"

Uncle Digger moved with more than his usual turtle speed. "Let me get my varmit gun."

Annalisa exchanged amused glances with Austin. Uncle Digger insisted on carrying a vintage rifle of some sort on the train in case of snakes, bears, cougars or other "varmits" as he called them. According to Miss Evelyn, he'd never fired a shot.

"You two go ahead," Austin said. "We'll clean up the leftovers."

As the older couple moved off into the woods, Annalisa replaced lids and rewrapped aluminum foil. Austin jammed paper plates and napkins into a plastic bag.

"I think they wanted to be alone."

"Yeah," Austin said. "Lovebirds at their ages. Who knew?"

"I think it's sweet and…kind of affirming."

He cocked his head. "What do you mean?"

"That love can ripen and grow with the years instead of dying out."

"Hmm" was all he said as he stared down at a bag of cookies, thoughtful.

A quiet broken only by birdsong and soft wind through the leaves stretched across the meadow. Annalisa thought of the way the older couple held hands as they'd sauntered into the trees.

Last night's kiss and now the romantic atmosphere of a picnic in the woods had her thinking things she probably shouldn't.

"Church was good," she ventured, opting for safer ground. "I'm glad you were there."

"Yeah."

"Will you go again?"

"I don't know. Maybe." He crushed a pop can in one hand. "Too many questions never get answered."

"I felt the same way until coming here. Your sister and Uncle Digger have changed my mind. God loves us, Austin, no matter what." Even if she struggled with guilt, she was learning the truth of God's grace and mercy. "I think God allowed me to go through some difficult times to bring me to this point."

"Are you saying God caused James to break your arm and hit you? To threaten you?" His face was a thundercloud. "What kind of God does that?"

If Austin knew the things she'd done out of loneliness and a heart devoid of direction, would he despise her? The question ate a hole in her wounded conscience. So many regrets.

"God didn't do those things, Austin. I stayed with James even though I knew he wasn't good for me. I can't blame God for my choices."

Austin's arms stiffened at his sides. His hands clenched into fists. She'd made him angry.

A memory flashed in her head, of fists and a livid face. Of James's temper.

Heart rattling, she pushed up from the quilt and walked quickly away and down the train tracks. She shouldn't be afraid, not of Austin. But James had programmed her to fear, had controlled her with his icy anger until she would do anything to avoid setting him off.

She hated living like this. Even though she'd moved far away, James still gripped her life.

Something gleamed in the gravel next to the iron railroad tracks. She stooped to discover an angled piece of flint sharp on one end and notched on the other.

"An arrowhead." Austin's voice came from over her shoulder. She turned to find him there, watching her with a solemn expression. "Natives hunted here, on this very spot, a long time ago. Long before there was a town or a railroad."

She rotated the stone in her fingers, a gray shiny remnant of the past.

"Are you okay?" The question he always asked, the one that melted her anxiety.

"I'm fine. Why?" But she knew, of course.

"I upset you."

She glanced around the glade, a pristine wilderness broken only by the train tracks.

"Only for a moment."

He eased an arm around her shoulders, let it lie there lightly as if gauging her acceptance. "You're safe with me."

"I know." And she did. In her head, she knew. In her heart, she knew. But bad experiences died hard.

When she didn't pull away, Austin drew her

close to his side and she rested there, letting tension drain away. Gently, he opened her fingers and touched the arrowhead, a gray gleam on her palm. "Quite a find. Rare and special. There aren't many left."

Like him. A rare and special find. A man to trust.

She was terrified of loving again, of taking a chance. If Austin knew everything about her past, would he reject her, as broken as she was?

"You're a beautiful woman, Annalisa," he said softly, his warm breath against her hair. "Inside and out."

If only he knew the truth....

It was then she decided to tell him, to put her past out in the open for him to reject or accept. Before her heart was too far gone.

"Remember that day at the falls?" she said, squeezing the arrowhead until the sharp edge cut into her skin. "You told me to trust you."

"As I recall you didn't have much choice."

"Maybe not, but you didn't let me down. You said I could trust you, and you told the truth." She drew a ragged breath. A squirrel scampered down a cottonwood tree, rustling leaves. "I, on the other hand, haven't always been honest with you."

She felt him tense and steeled herself for his rejection.

"Is this about your relationship with James?"

"Yes, in a way. But in another way, James was the culmination of a lot of mistakes I made."

"We all make mistakes."

"Not like mine." She twisted the arrowhead, clenching and unclenching. Grief of her own making rose in her throat and tingled behind her eyelids. "Remember when I said I had no family left? That isn't true. I have a sister."

"Olivia. But I thought…" He stepped away to look at her, head tilted in bewilderment.

"You thought she died—and I let you believe it."

"Why?" His brow furrowed. "Why would you do that?"

She parked her fists on her hips and gazed upward. Cotton-white clouds gazed back, benevolent. "In a way, she's lost to me. We don't talk. I haven't seen her in…a long time."

"Want to tell me why?"

No, but she must. "When Grandpa died, Olivia and I disagreed over the distribution of his farm and property. That's about the time James came along. I was so stupid. I know that now, but then I was blinded by James's take-charge charm. He said he wanted to take care of me, for me not to worry. He'd handle everything."

"What kind of things?"

"Everything, Austin, everything, although I

didn't understand at the time that he wanted absolute possession of my life. I thought his possessiveness was a sign of love." She brushed her hair behind an ear, wishing she hadn't been so needy and unwise. "Olivia wanted to keep the farm. James considered it an albatross. Cash was better, he claimed, to start fresh with him in California. Olivia was trying to tie me down, break us up."

And to her shame, she'd agreed, choosing James and his false attention over her family and the little farm that had molded her childhood.

"So you sold out?"

She dropped her head, stared at a twig stuck beneath her shoelace. "I wanted to please James."

"Didn't Olivia have a say?"

"Not legally." Tears gathered in her eyes. To cover the emotion, she crouched and plucked away the twig. "Grandpa trusted me to do the right thing. He trusted *me,* and I let him down. I let Olivia down. She said she'd never forgive me, and I haven't spoken to her since."

"Have you tried?"

She tilted her head to look up at him, standing tall and calm in front of her. "A couple of times. She hung up on me."

He crouched with her and touched her hands. "I'm sorry."

"I keep praying, asking the Lord to forgive me and show me a way to make amends."

"How's *that* working for you?" He offered a crooked, cynical smile.

"Not so well." She lifted her shoulders, sighed. "But why should He? When I sold out Olivia, I sold Him out, too. I traded everything for a charming man who told me pretty lies, who insisted he was all I needed to be happy. I didn't need my sister. I didn't need God. All I needed was James."

"Annalisa," Austin said softly.

She pushed to a stand, not deserving the acceptance in his expression. He didn't know the worst.

"Did you know I turned my back on God for him? James claimed my church took up too much time, that he couldn't bear to be away from me that much."

At the time, she'd viewed James's desire to be with her as a sign of his love. And she'd been so needy and broken that she'd traded the true love of the Father for a man who saw her as a possession.

The ugly truth that was her life festered to breaking point. She spun away as angry tears burst free. In a broken voice, she said, "I gave him everything, Austin. *Everything.* How can God forgive me for that? And in return, I got exactly what I deserved—a man who humiliated me, controlled me, used me."

"And tried to kill you."

She heard the disgust in his voice. Now that Austin knew the whole story, he would walk away and never look back. He'd see her for the damaged, broken human being she was.

She moved away from him, deeper into the woods. The sharp scents of fertile earth and decaying leaves rose, stirred by her feet. The train had stopped on a forested ridge and now she broke through the oaks and sweet gums to the incline leading down into a vast valley of colorful timber. The sights were glorious, but her shame was too deep to focus. She'd thought she was healing, that her time with good, decent, salt-of-the-earth people like Cassie and the Parsonses and Austin had brought her back to a point of peace and grace.

How long would regret hold her captive?

"Annalisa."

She turned to find him standing there, a cowboy in a white hat, with a stricken face. She raised her chin. "I thought you should know what kind of woman's been living under your roof."

"I do know." She heard the swish of denim as his long legs crossed the space that separated them in three strides. "Grief causes people to do things they wouldn't ordinarily do."

She blinked, not comprehending. "What?"

"You loved your grandfather."

"More than anyone other than my sister."

"You grieved his loss."

"I felt as if my anchor was gone."

"And that's when James stepped right in."

She stared at him, stunned. "Are you saying that James took advantage of the situation?"

"What do you think?"

She thought he might be right. She prayed he was right.

"I don't want to be a terrible person." She averted her face. He reached out, took her chin and turned her back to face him.

"Don't do this to yourself. I've known terrible people and you're not one of them."

When her lips trembled, his chest rose and fell in a deep sigh. Then, he pulled her into his arms. Head resting against the steady beat of his heart, Annalisa slipped her arms around his waist and held on tight.

"Listen to me, Annalisa. Any man worth his salt would know how special and good and decent you are."

She shook her head, struggling to deny his words. "No—"

"Shh. Yes. Yes, he would. A decent man wouldn't take advantage. He wouldn't expect you to give up your family and your faith. He would care about what you care about." He stroked the hair from her damp cheek, tilted her face and kissed her forehead. "James was a fool for not knowing how blessed he was to have you."

And Annalisa knew then why his opinion mattered so very, very much. She was completely, totally, wondrously in love with Austin Blackwell.

Chapter Fourteen

Austin held Annalisa close, grateful that she'd trusted him enough to share her pain. And in the same breath, he cursed himself a fool for not sharing his.

She didn't get it, didn't understand that he was far more tainted than anything she had ever done. And he dared not tell her. Not now, not after he'd given his fancy speech about worthy men. Annalisa had been lied to and abused by a man who professed to love her. If she knew the circumstances of Blair's death, she would look at him with revulsion and fear, and she would run. She'd assume him guilty as others had, even though he'd never hurt anyone other than himself.

He felt a tug deep inside, in the place where his spirit once had reached up to God. The spot ached to lean on Someone stronger than himself. But God had let him down in his darkest hour and like Annalisa, he struggled to trust again. But he wanted to. Oh, how he wanted to.

He stroked a ranch-roughened hand over Annalisa's hair, down her slender back, enchanted by her softness. She cuddled into him, and he felt strong and manly and full of emotions he couldn't voice. Every primal instinct to protect and defend flooded him like the gush of Whisper Falls.

He thought about the things she'd told him, about her sister and grandfather, about her ex. The idea that James had taken advantage of a sad, grieving, lonely woman boiled up red-hot inside him. Not just any woman, Annalisa. His sweet, beautiful Annalisa.

He wanted to make all kinds of promises, promises he'd die trying to keep. But he'd made promises before and come away empty and beaten. The truth was he didn't have all the answers. He only knew he'd fallen in love with Annalisa, a foolish thing to do, and yet, he was happy. For years, he'd awakened each morning to go through the motions of a lonely, empty life. Now, he awoke with anticipation, eager for the day because of her.

With the smell of autumn and Annalisa's sweet perfume swirling in his senses, Austin squeezed his eyes shut as a half-formed plan drifted through his head. No one in Whisper Falls knew about Blair. No one but Cassie.

Annalisa lifted her head and kissed his chin. A thrill ran through him. He sighed, stroked her cheek, her jaw, her lips and then he kissed her, full on the mouth, and she kissed him back, raising on tiptoes to twine her slender arms around his neck and tug him closer.

He had no armor against this woman.

He wanted to be with her, to go on feeling this happiness. And the only way to make that happen was to be sure she never learned the truth about his wife.

Annalisa rubbed the pale skin of her left arm, intrigued by how the muscle had shrunken in only six weeks. With a happy smile, she spritzed window cleaner on the windshield of her latest addition—a dandy little used car.

Accessing her checking account had been easier than she'd expected. With the help of an understanding Whisper Falls banker, all her assets had been electronically transferred to a new account. Her greatest worry had been James, but as Austin reminded her, James already knew where she was. Accessing her account wouldn't alert him to anything except that she was now standing on her own two feet.

"What do you think, boys?" she said to the two big dogs sniffing the tires and checking out the strange vehicle. Hoss wagged his tail and nudged her arm.

"You don't care about cars. You want a head rub."

She gave him one, thinking of how satisfied and happy she felt today.

Thank goodness she'd had sense enough not to share her accounts jointly with James, although following one of his recent manipulative outbursts, she'd told him she would. She could almost hear his voice. "I don't want you to worry about money. Leave that to me. Math isn't your strong suit." And the worst, "Sometimes I think you don't love me at all."

He'd made her feel as though he couldn't live without her, as though his need for control was actually deep and passionate love. He had made her believe *she* was lacking because she desired a life apart from him.

And she'd fallen for his twisted manipulation every time except for the bank account. Thank goodness. Even when she'd turned away from her Heavenly Father, He was still looking out for her.

"What a mighty God we serve," she muttered. God had led her here to this loving place where she could heal and find her bearings.

The idea of finally being her own woman again sent a burst of energy through her system. The Lord had forgiven her, this town had embraced her and she was as safe here as she'd ever be. She was almost convinced James would never bother her again.

Only the break with her sister remained to plague her conscience. She'd tried again to make contact. Tried and failed. Olivia had changed her phone number.

Annalisa figured she was the reason for the change. Little sister never wanted to hear from her again.

"Slick ride," Austin said, coming out the back door to where she was parked. Hoss immediately abandoned Annalisa, rushing to Austin's side with an eager doggy smile. She understood. She'd rather be with Austin, too.

"I bought her this morning. Isn't she great? A little dusty and in need of a tune up, but Tommy down at the Busted Knuckle Garage said she had a lot of good miles left in her."

"Tommy knows cars. Where did you find it?" He walked around the back, leaned down, looked underneath.

Annalisa released an inner breath. Austin hadn't criticized. He'd not chastised her for buying the car without his approval. Satisfaction glowed through her. She rubbed the windshield a little harder.

"It belonged to Mayor Fairchild's grandma.

She hasn't driven since she went into the nursing home." Annalisa gave the side mirror a spritz and shine. "You and Cassie and the Parsonses won't have to be at my beck and call anymore."

Austin ran a palm along the front fender. "We didn't mind."

"I know and I'm grateful, but it's time for me to take care of myself again, to remember that I can."

Steady green eyes rested on her face. Her pulse fluttered.

"How does it feel?"

She grinned up at him. "Really good, thanks to you." His support had given her much-needed confidence. "Want to go for a spin?"

"Don't you have work?"

"We have time for a quick ride. Hop in."

When he folded his long legs into the small compact, they both laughed. Austin shot her a wry look. "Snug fit."

With a light heart, she drove him down the road and back. The little compact zipped along without a sputter. "Great gas mileage, too."

"You got a deal on this baby," he said with a pat to the dashboard.

Annalisa felt as if she'd burst with pride. It was ridiculous how much his compliment meant. James would have whined that she should have let him pick out the car, that she couldn't make that kind of decision by herself, that buying a car on her own meant she didn't trust him.

But it was time to forget James. Forget the past and move forward.

She pulled the little white car close to the porch. Austin unwound long legs and pried himself from the seat, then came around to the driver's-side window and leaned in. "Mind if I come by the Iron Horse later?"

"I'll be disappointed if you don't."

A slow smile lifted the corners of his eyes.

Annalisa tugged at his shirt sleeve, still smiling up at him with expectation. He didn't let her down. His tall form bent low, he kissed her once, then again, lingering until her breath shortened and her pulse rattled madly.

Curious, Jet raised his paws up to the window opening and jammed his massive black head between them. Annalisa jerked back against the headrest with a snort as Austin pushed the dog away. "Get down, you crazy dog."

Jet didn't take offense. He plopped on his bottom and pawed at Austin's jeans, whining.

"Didn't know we had a canine chaperone," Austin said, grinning. "You'd better get going before we both get in trouble."

Annalisa laughed and rolled up the window. With a final wave, she pulled away and headed for the Iron Horse, mood light and happy.

* * *

Austin stood in the yard with Hoss and Jet, and watched Annalisa spin down the driveway in her dandy little compact. She'd changed in the weeks he'd known her. Changes for the good. She no longer jumped when he raised his voice or when the telephone rang. And now, she'd bought a car. She was looking at apartments, too, and he knew she'd soon be gone from the ranch.

He was okay with that, or at least he told himself he was. He could still look out for her. They could still be friends.

He removed his hat and ran a hand through his hair. Friends. Who was he kidding? He'd kissed her. She'd kissed him back, the look in her eyes pulling him in, giving him hope. They were more than friends.

Could a man and woman build a relationship when one was less than honest?

He'd done some praying lately and gotten exactly what he'd expected. Nothing.

"Come on, boys," he said, replacing the hat with an unnecessary shove. "We got work to do."

A few hours later, he brushed and dried Cisco's glossy coat and turned him loose in the pasture, the cows successfully moved to new grazing land for the coming winter. Clouds gathered in the west, banking up the promise of much-needed rain and probably cooler temps. Winter was coming, all right.

Overhead, a flock of geese honked, drawing the dogs' attention. Jet went crazy, leaping into the air as if he could pull one down. Hoss, who loved cattle but had no interest in game, gazed at his friend in mild amusement. At least, Austin thought the old shepherd seemed amused. Maybe he'd been alone too long.

Annalisa had changed some of that aloneness. She'd drawn him out into the community and even with the fear of others learning about Blair's death, he enjoyed the new friends.

"Annalisa." He said her name aloud, softly, liking the feel of it on his lips.

He gazed up at the huge V-shaped flock, hoping Annalisa didn't share their urge for a warmer climate.

A spiral of dust rose from the curve in the road leading to his ranch. He watched it grow larger, aware that just about any car driving down that road would be coming to his place. Hoss and Jet trotted out to the driveway, expectant.

A late-model sports car, flashy red and laced with chrome, roared into his yard and a man stepped out. Dressed in dark slacks, a yellow pullover and fancy loafers, the stranger looked out of place.

Austin had never seen this guy in his life, but

the hairs on the back of his neck prickled. "Hello, there, are you lost?"

The blond man, a bodybuilder type with wide shoulders and powerful arms, speared him with a glare. "Are you Blackwell?"

"I am. Who's asking?"

Popeye arms fisted on slender hips. "Where's Annalisa?"

Austin's blood froze in his veins. This had to be James Winchell.

He battled to keep his expression bland. "Who?"

"Don't play dumb with me. I know she's staying here. With you." He spat the last words, accusing.

Austin hackled. His fists flexed. "I live here with my sister. What do you want with this Annalisa woman, whoever she is?"

"Don't play me for a fool, Blackwell. I'm smarter than either of you give me credit for. I know she's living here. I even know about her pathetic little job at a snack shop." He spat the words as if they tasted nasty.

Not good. Not good at all.

"Don't know what you're talking about, buddy, but I suggest you take your problems elsewhere."

"I'll tell you what I'm talking about." The man jabbed a finger toward Austin's face. "Annalisa took what's mine and I aim to get it back. And no ignorant cowpoke is going to stand in my way. She owes me."

Heat rose up the back of Austin's neck. He fought the urge to shove his fist through James's smirk. "I think you have that backward. She doesn't owe you anything. Go back to your life. Leave her alone."

Shrewd eyes, hard as blue glass, glinted daggers. In the distance, thunder rumbled. "Why? So you can have her?"

Austin clamped his lips into a tight line. So much for staying cool. "Look, man. I don't know you, but I do know what you did to Annalisa. She wants no part of you."

James mottled red, the veins in his neck extending. His lips twisted in a sneer of disgust. "I should have known she'd latch on to the first man that looked at her. She's like that. Has to have a man to take care of her."

He made a motion toward Austin. Austin took a step back. He didn't dare punch a cop. But he wanted to. Badly.

Beside him, Jet let out a soft growl, his black fur bristling. Hoss edged closer to his master, expression alert and concerned. Austin dropped a hand to each noble head.

"Easy, boys." To James, he said, "I don't think my dogs like you. I suggest you hit the trail before they get nervous and do something you'll regret."

James eased back, but his tight-jawed determi-

nation didn't lessen. "What are you go.
Kill me? The way you killed your *wife?*"

A fist of fear encircled Austin's windpipe, cutting off all his air. The thing he'd feared had come to life. James was a cop and he knew about Blair.

Shock and anxiety must have shown on Austin's face because James's defensive stance changed. His expression grew knowing and predatory. He leaned in. "You didn't tell her, did you? Annalisa doesn't know."

Austin thought of all the chances he'd had to come clean with Annalisa, but fear of losing her had held him back. He should have told her. He wished he had.

"Well, well, well, cowboy. What do you have to say now? Cat got your tongue?" Like a predator in for the kill, James saw his advantage and pressed in, his smile cruelly pleased. "Annalisa doesn't know she's sleeping with a murderer. Now, isn't that an interesting little tidbit?"

Austin lurched toward the intruder. Jet barked. Hoss growled. His head screamed a reminder not to put his hands on a cop, not to assault an officer of the law. Not again.

Through gritted teeth and more self-control than he dreamed possible, he pushed his face into James's and growled, "Get…off…my…land!"

With the upper body strength of a steroid user, James shoved him backward. Austin stumbled, his boots awkward and heavy. He thought of those powerful arms and hands on Annalisa, hurting her, and anger charged through him like electricity. He shook with the urge to retaliate.

God help me. Help me be strong for her. Show me what to do.

Drawing on every fiber of self-control he had, Austin stepped away and let James win.

The thunder rumbled closer, clouds darkening with each passing minute.

James smiled his cocky, mirthless smile. "You're not dealing with Annalisa anymore, cowboy. You're dealing with a man with the power to make you crawl. So let me give you fair warning. If you like your freedom, stay out of my way."

Executing a mock salute, Annalisa's tormentor—and now Austin's—got into his sports car and roared away.

A chill ran down Austin's spine. He knew exactly where James Winchell was headed.

Chapter Fifteen

Humming softly, Annalisa slid four of Miss Evelyn's frozen pies into the oven and set the timer.

"Do you think four is enough for the rest of the day?" she asked Uncle Digger.

In his usual blue-and-gold hat and striped overalls, Uncle Digger motioned toward the store room. "If not, Evelyn has more in the freezer."

She knew that, but she didn't like to keep customers waiting. Or worse, have them leave without buying anything. The Iron Horse did all right, but according to the owners, business had improved with Annalisa at the counter. Even though suspecting they were being kind, she nonetheless wanted to prove her worth.

This little snack shop in Whisper Falls was a far cry from her former life, but she loved it. She loved the people, the work, her new car and most of all, she loved Austin Blackwell. If she wasn't mistaken, he loved her, too, though something held him back.

But she was in no rush. Not this time, not after the mistakes she'd made. As her arm had healed, so had her heart and soul. This time, she'd take her time, let love grow and learn who God intended her to be along the way.

She prayed that Austin's wounds, whatever they might be, would also heal. She touched her lips, remembered the sweet way he'd kissed her goodbye and thought of the old adage that love heals all wounds.

"Where is everyone today?" she asked. A handful of customers lined the counter, but the shop was quieter than normal.

"I think we're in for a storm this evening," Uncle Digger said, "but business is always slow after the Pumpkin Fest."

She could tell the situation worried him. It worried her, too. Without business, the Iron Horse had no need of her.

"When will it pick up again?"

He rubbed his mustache, his white eyebrows dipping. "Generally lasts until Christmas, but Evelyn's steaming up new ways to get folks here through Thanksgiving. Chamber's kind of lagging, but she'll stoke a fire in their coal bin."

Salt shakers clattered as she grouped them for refills. "Any ideas yet?"

"Some silly notion about getting play actors to hold up the train. Something like Jesse James." He shook his head. "I can't get on board with that one."

Annalisa unscrewed shaker lids and hid a smile. She was coming to love this odd little man with his train comments. "There has to be something that would attract visitors in the off season."

"Speaking of attracting things." Uncle Digger hitched the straps of his overalls. "I noticed a few sparks between you and Austin. How's that working out?"

"He's a good man."

Austin was more than a good man. He was the man she wanted in her future. For the first time in a long time, life was good. Eventually, she might even stop looking over her shoulder expecting James to burst in and ruin everything.

"Uncle Digger, could I ask you something?"

"Anything at all. Even if I don't know the answer, I know Him who does." They were interrupted when several customers came to the cash register. Uncle Digger, in his usual half-speed mode, rang them up.

Annalisa topped off the salt shakers. The timer on the heating unit tinged. Grabbing a hot pad, she removed a sub sandwich and wrapped the Philly cheese for the local barber. "Anything else for you, Sid?"

The barber, whose head was as clean as a cue ball, answered, "This will do for now. Got to get back to the shop."

"Clipping a lot of ears, are you, Sid?" Uncle Digger asked as he took the man's money.

"Not near enough."

Uncle Digger nodded sagely. "Hold tight to the rails, son, and keep looking up. Whisper Falls is on the rise. This time next spring we'll be on the gravy train. Just you wait and see."

With a wave, Sid exited the Iron Horse, and several other customers soon followed. She was left with only the two coffee drinkers at the counter. Annalisa topped off their cups and put the carafe back on the heater.

With her customers taken care of for the moment, Annalisa returned to Uncle Digger. Idly, he took a wet cloth and began wiping down the work station. Uncle Digger had one speed. But Annalisa knew his thinking was anything but slow.

"Now, what's on your mind, missy? Wouldn't be that cowboy, would it?"

She fought a blush, gave up and let it heat her face. Was she that obvious?

Austin pulled into the parking area outside the train depot with his heart on his sleeve and a vise around his heart. One quick look around allayed his first concern. No fancy red sports car. With his knowledge of back roads, he'd easily beaten James into town, but he didn't have long. Winchell was the kind of man who would stop at nothing to get what he wanted. And he wanted to make Annalisa pay for leaving him.

Austin was certain, from the dark look in the man's eyes that he hadn't come to Whisper Falls out of love. He'd come for revenge.

Annalisa was in danger, both from James and from the truth Austin carried inside him like a rattlesnake.

He had no choice. He had to tell her about Blair and about the charges before James did. She would hate him for the lie, she might even fear him, but he would not allow James the pleasure of throwing that ugly surprise in her face.

He nodded to the town barber as he hurried inside the Iron Horse. His heart skipped a beat when he saw her behind the counter, talking with Uncle Digger. She looked up when the door snapped shut behind him.

"Austin!" Pleasure sparkled in her eyes. Her lips curved.

An answering joy touched Austin for a moment, but he didn't smile. He couldn't, knowing he was about to erase that look from her face forever.

Worried that James could burst through the door any minute, he hurried around behind the counter with grim determination. Both Annalisa and Uncle Digger stared at him curiously. A coffee drinker tossed some change on the counter and left.

"James is in town," he blurted.

Annalisa choked out a small, distressed noise and turned as white as the shop's coffee mugs. She clapped her hands over her mouth, eyes wide with shock.

Uncle Digger frowned, looking from Austin to Annalisa and back. "Who is James, and why is Annalisa afraid of him?"

Austin gave him a quick overview.

Digger's reply came fast. "Take her and go home. I'll send that feller flying."

Austin softened at the older man's determined look. Uncle Digger cared for Annalisa. He'd protect her if he could, but sooner or later, James would get to her.

With a strength that surprised him, Austin said, "Running won't solve the problem."

The truth of his own statement hit him between the eyes. Hadn't his family said the same thing to him? Yet, he'd run away from Texas, and look what good that had done him. Six years of hiding on his ranch as if he was guilty. Six years of being alone, of refusing to face the past. Six years of barely living.

He didn't want Annalisa to live that way. If there was to be a showdown with James, better to get it over with now. Then, and only then, could she hope to move on.

Austin hurt to know that she would likely move on without him.

Gently, lovingly, with his stomach tied in knots, he gripped Annalisa's shoulders and stared into her beautiful sweet eyes, willing her to hear his heart and understand.

"Maybe James will come here and maybe he won't," he said. "I figure he will. But either way, you and I have to talk. Now."

Uncle Digger picked up the urgency. He clapped Austin's shoulder once. "You two talk. I got things to do." And then he shuffled through the door leading into the museum.

He was no more than out of sight when Annalisa gripped Austin's forearms and said, "I don't want to see him. Where is he? Did you talk to him?"

Her voice shook, and Austin thought he'd break in two.

"He came to the ranch. I don't know how he found it, but he did." Cops have ways. They even know things that aren't true. "He said you owed him and that he'd find you."

She sucked in a nervous breath. "Does he know I work here?"

As much as he despised adding to her fear, the truth was all that mattered now. She had to know. "He seemed to."

"Of course he knows. He always knows. He's a cop, a relentless investigator." She twisted her fingers together. "I should have left. I should have gone far, far away when he first called, but I…"

Austin's pulse thundered. Hope flared, then sputtered and died. She'd stayed because of him. And now he was about to destroy the fledgling love growing between them.

Hearing the crack and splinter of his own heart, he took her hands in his. Swallowing hard, he said, "I have to tell you something about myself. Something bad. James knows, and he'll use it to hurt us both."

Annalisa stilled, blue eyes raking his face. "This is about Blair, isn't it?"

He blanched, eyes dropping shut. The blinding pain of yesterday's mistakes tore at him like tiger's teeth "Yes. My…wife."

She slid her hands into his and squeezed, willing him to look at her. "I know she died. What happened? Was she ill?"

He heard the terrible hope in her voice. She was smart. She suspected the truth would be too much to bear.

But love without truth was doomed to die. Better now than later.

"Yes, she was sick, but not in the way you mean. She had emotional problems."

Again, that stillness before she murmured, "Did you love her?"

He gazed down at Annalisa's fine-boned hands in his, remembering Blair. Remembering the love-hate relationship they'd shared. "I tried. I thought love could fix her, and most of the time she was fine. But not always."

How did he explain the confused, mistrusting woman he'd married?

"She was abused as a child." His throat tightened with the horror. "In ways I can't even think about. She never resolved those issues. Sometimes she hated me. Sometimes she loved me. Sometimes she'd disappear for days, saying she needed space."

"I'm sorry."

He blew out a soft sigh. "I didn't know what to do. I was young and embarrassed. I lied to people, told them she'd gone to visit friends or made other excuses. Those lies came back to haunt me."

"Did you know where she went?"

"No. Never." But there were those who didn't believe him. Would she? "People gossiped. They said she cheated on me."

"Did she?"

He shrugged, although he was feeling anything but casual. The old emasculating pain rose up in his chest, hot and tight. He hadn't been enough to keep his bride at home. "I didn't want to know.

But sometimes I was so angry at her. We fought a lot."

"What happened? How did she…die?" The last word was whispered, as if she knew Blair's death was out of the ordinary.

A swirl of images invaded Austin's head. Bile rose in his throat at the memories. He swallowed, fought to tell her everything. "Police found her in a motel room over a hundred miles from home. She'd been…murdered."

Annalisa's body sagged in shock. "Oh, Austin. What you must have gone through."

He'd gone through more than she could ever know. Regardless of Blair's behavior, he'd cared for her. Maybe in the end the love had died, but once upon a time when he'd believed in happy ever after, he had loved his wife.

"I'll never forget that knock on my door. The police cars in the driveway." The scene was imprinted on his brain, branding him a failure. Two black-and-whites and an unmarked car. The group of officers whose compassion was hidden behind a veil of suspicion. The ham sandwich he had left on the counter. "She'd been gone for ten days that time. The police wanted to know why I hadn't reported her missing."

"Why hadn't you?"

"She always came back. I just thought…" He lifted one shoulder, as helpless now as he was then. In truth, he hadn't wanted to know where Blair disappeared to. He'd been afraid of what he might discover.

"I'd lied. Told everyone she'd gone to visit friends. The police found that suspicious."

He loosened his hold on Annalisa to run a weary hand down his face. Anything to wipe away the nightmare. "They wouldn't let me bury her. Not for a long time. By the time they released her, I couldn't go to her funeral."

"Why?"

The horror of those days filled his head and heart. If not for his family, for Cassie and his mother and dad, he might have done something crazy.

"They found bruises and evidence of past abuse. With no other suspects, the trail led straight to the unhappy husband." He blew out a nervous breath and blurted the rest. "I was in jail, arrested…and charged with murder."

Chapter Sixteen

Annalisa sucked in a gasp, stunned by the revelation. Austin? Accused of murder?

For a long moment, she stared at him, stomach churning. Was Austin capable of hurting the woman he was supposed to love and cherish forever? Had she fallen in love with another violent man?

The notion chilled her to the soul.

How did she reconcile the tender cowboy with a man accused of murder?

Her head spun. Blood roared through her temples. Nothing made sense. She needed to think.

After a few agonizing seconds while she said nothing, Austin dropped his head and turned away.

She opened her mouth. Closed it. She had no idea what to say, but she couldn't let him just walk out of her life. There had to be an explanation. There had to be.

She reached out to call him back so he could explain and help her understand.

But at that moment, the Iron Horse door slammed open, reverberating on its hinges. Words froze on Annalisa's tongue.

James Winchell strode into the room.

He brushed past Austin, slanting an arrogant smirk in the cowboy's direction. Annalisa wasn't sure whether to run or fight, but one thing she knew for certain, she needed Austin.

"Austin." She heard the tremble in her voice.

"Forget him." James strutted toward her, a confident smile on his face, a face as cold as it was charming. "Hello, doll. Miss me?"

Her knees began to shake, stomach threatening to reject the sandwich she'd had for lunch. She licked lips gone dry as sand. He was as handsome as ever, slick and polished and confident. And he scared her senseless.

"Lord Jesus," she prayed silently. *"Help me be strong."*

Until now, until Austin and Whisper Falls, she'd not had the strength to stand against him. Somehow, with God's help, this time she would.

"James." The name came out in a nervous whisper as if she was a child caught in misbehaving.

"I missed you, doll. Get your stuff and let's roll out of this dump."

She shook her head, clenching her hands behind

her back to hide the shakes. She would not let him do this to her again. She would not. Stiffening her spine, she said, "Go back to California, James."

"Not without you." He smiled, but no pleasure lit his eyes. She'd never realized that before. For all his charm, his smiles, his wily words, his eyes had always been hard and empty when they looked at her. Not tender like Austin's.

She flashed a look at the cowboy, his name on her lips. "Austin, don't go. Please."

He never hesitated. Even though she knew she'd hurt him with her silence, he was beside her in an instant, solid, stalwart, a refuge of strength that made her more determined than ever to break free of James Winchell.

"So it's you again. The cowboy," James sneered. "If you know what's good for you, you'll get lost and stay lost."

Annalisa eyed the vein in James's neck—the one that pulsed when he was upset. It pulsed now, bulging with contained rage. For a split second, she relived the snap and pain of a broken arm and shuddered to know what he could do if he chose.

"Leave us alone, James."

"Not a chance, babe. You're mine." He lifted his palms in a gesture of placation. She'd seen him use it with suspects, a false manipulative gesture to get his way. Voice soft and deceptively sweet, he said, "I've come all this way to tell you you're forgiven. Come home now and everything will be just like it was before."

He flashed the cold, chilling smile again. Annalisa's blood curdled the way it had that awful day at Whisper Falls.

"I can't. I don't want to." She backed away from him, a mistake that revealed her anxiety.

His face hardened. "I think you'll want to reconsider." Viselike fingers snaked out and manacled her wrist. "Now, let's go before I get angry."

"Get your hands off the lady." The words were spoken quietly, but the underlying steel in Austin's tone left no doubt he meant what he said. His gaze was locked on James. Like two tigers engaged in mortal battle, the men glared.

James's fingers tightened until her wrist bones ached. A flash of his furious strength had her knees knocking and her mouth too dry to swallow.

Surely, he wouldn't hurt her here in front of anyone. His abuse had always been subtle and private and easily covered up. The broken arm had been a terrible loss of his usual control and even then, he'd done the deed in private, on a deserted road far off the beaten path. He hadn't expected her to bolt. He'd thought she'd come whimpering back the way she'd always done and he would have told everyone that she, clumsy thing, had fallen.

"I warned you, cowboy, don't interfere between a man and his fiancée."

"I'm not your fiancée." Teeth gritted, she jerked hard against him but couldn't break his grip. "Let me go."

James narrowed his eyes, nostrils flared. "You've developed some spunk. I don't think I like it."

Adrenaline pumping, Annalisa surveyed the snack shop and found the room empty. Her heart sank. At the first sign of trouble the Iron Horse occupants had disappeared. Like everyone else in her life, friends faded away when times got hard.

No, not everyone. She flashed a look at the one person still in the room.

Austin, her Austin. He hadn't moved. He stood quietly, boots planted wide, arms loose at his sides. Only the grim line of his mouth—that wonderful mouth that kissed with such tenderness— indicated the depth of his emotion.

Austin hadn't abandoned her. She stared into his beloved face, willing him to meet her gaze.

He couldn't have killed his wife. He couldn't have.

Finally, his eyes flicked to hers, caught and held on for a long, meaningful second as if he had opened his soul and let her in. In those green depths she read sorrow laced with love.

Austin loved her.

He blinked, and the moment evaporated, a wisp of smoke on the wind.

And just as quickly, Austin sprang like a coiled snake, shoving between her and James. Caught off guard, James stumbled backward. Annalisa tore her wrist from his grasp. The bones ached but she paid them no mind. She'd suffered worse.

She braced herself, waiting for his cold rage to burn red-hot. She took three steps back, bumped the counter with her hip, thankful to God for Austin's broad shoulders between her and the abuser who claimed to love her.

What a sick, sick view of love.

James's face had grown purple with anger. Austin's was simply determined.

Fright and faith warred inside her. Fear of James. Faith in Austin. And in God to protect them both as he'd done that day behind Whisper Falls.

But Austin was outmatched against James's superior training. He was in danger, too.

Annalisa stiffened her resolve. Making a clean break from the past was her responsibility, not Austin's. No matter what James said or what he did, this time she would stand her ground.

She moved in beside the cowboy and touched his hand. His fingers twitched, but he never took his eyes off James.

Gathering her nerve, she said, "You should leave now, James. It's over between us."

"It's not over until I say it is."

"You heard the lady. She'd not interested."

James took a step forward, his icy glare confident. "You should come with me before your boyfriend gets hurt."

"That's not happening." The voice came from behind her.

Annalisa swiveled her head as Uncle Digger appeared through the door of the museum, hefting a coal shovel.

James sneered. "No old man scares me."

"What about the rest of us?" Davis Turner entered the room, a hammer in one hand. Behind him came Sid, the barber, with his shears. And behind him were Cassie and Louise, each hairdresser wielding a heavy iron straightener. Pudge Loggins from the bait and tackle shop was next, toting an oar over one shoulder. Next came Creed Carter and Mayor Fairchild, armed with nothing but determination.

"Chief Farnsworth's been notified," Rusty said.

As she watched, astonished and humbled, the small snack shop filled with townspeople who lined up beside Austin with the tools of their trade in hand, ready to protect and defend.

Tears sprang to Annalisa's eyes. This town cared about her. *Her.* The woman who'd stumbled and fallen too many times. They'd accepted her anyway. And Austin, too. This funny little town of quirky mountain folks were the family and love she'd been looking for since Grandpa died. At the warmth of that love, every fear melted away like snowflakes in June.

But even when he was outnumbered James was not the kind of man to back down.

"Do you people know what kind of man you're standing alongside?"

"Leave it, Winchell." Austin's voice carried a threat.

"Oh, you'd like that, wouldn't you? Then you could go right on fooling these people the way you fooled the Texas justice system."

All the strength went out of Annalisa's legs. She grabbed for the back of a nearby chair. James knew about Austin's past. The secret he'd hidden from everyone in this room, even her.

She understood now. Blair's death had broken him, and the accusation of murder had forced him to leave everything he knew and loved to come to the remote Ozarks where no one knew. She of all people understood how much that anonymity meant.

To have his past revealed again would shatter him.

"James, please." Desperate to spare Austin the humiliation, she forced her legs to move the six steps toward James. "I'll go with you. Just don't say any more."

"No!" Austin's cry splintered through her. He caught her elbow but she shook him off and continued forward like a programmed robot.

"Let's go home, James." Her lips were tight, her face frozen, her insides dead. "Take me home. I want to go home. With you."

The last phrase choked her, but she'd do anything to protect Austin. None of this was his fault. He shouldn't bear the brunt of James's wrath.

She reached out to James, but his lip curled in disgust. He pushed her hands away as if her touch dirtied him.

"Too late, doll. I don't want you anymore. You've made your bed with scum, now sleep in it. But before I shake the dust off this dump, these folks are going to hear the truth about your cowboy."

And with more sadistic pleasure than she'd thought possible, he told them.

Austin felt the world tilt and knew the quiet life he'd built in Whisper Falls was coming to an end. James spewed his vitriol for everyone to hear, twisting the facts for the worst presentation. By the time he finished, a satisfied smirk on his lips, Austin had not only murdered his wife, he'd abused her for years and hidden her away for days so his crimes wouldn't be suspected. James left nothing out. Not the fights with police officers, not the condition of Blair's battered body, not the sensational trial full of circumstantial evidence, nor the controversial verdict when Austin had walked away a free man.

It made him sick to his stomach.

In defeat, Austin gazed around the room at the shocked faces of his neighbors and the people he'd almost thought of as friends.

"That's not true," Cassie cried. "Austin loved his wife. She was mentally ill. She did irrational things—"

James interrupted. "You're his sister. Naturally, you'd take his side. You were probably an accomplice. I hear you were widowed on your honeymoon and the unfortunate groom had nice life insurance. Just like your brother's wife."

Cassie's wounded gasp ripped through Austin. His blood boiled. She didn't deserve the brunt of Winchell's venom. "Shut up, Winchell. Leave her out of this. Everyone in this room knows Cassie's story."

"But they didn't know yours, did they?"

What could he say? They hadn't. He hung his head like a bronc rider knocked in the dirt, breathless.

By day's end, everyone in Whisper Falls would know his ugliest secret. He'd be an outcast again, a man under suspicion of murdering his wife, a man who couldn't even go to the grocery store without stares and whispers burning his ears.

Gut tight with shame, he did the only thing he could, the thing he'd come to do. Protect Annalisa once and for all.

"Annalisa is the important one here. And no matter what you say or do to me, I won't let you hurt her again. Get out of this town and don't come back. Don't call, don't write, don't visit."

"Or what, Blackwell? You gonna kill me?"

James had him at a disadvantage and he knew it. Truth was Austin couldn't stop a man who didn't want to be stopped. But he could try.

Fists tight, he took a step toward James. To his amazement, a dozen feet shuffled on tile as everyone in the room stepped up with him.

He glanced to his left and then to his right. Uncle Digger nodded once. His mustache quivered indignantly. "We stand by our own."

A mumble of agreement passed down the line of townspeople.

James, who'd clearly expected the opposite results, narrowed his eyes into slits. The pleased smirk changed to incredulity. "Are you people crazy? You have a murderer in your midst."

"Folks around here *are* a little crazy, mister," Uncle Digger said, tapping the handle of his shovel. "Mostly, we're crazy about each other.

We're a peace-loving town, but you ain't proved to appreciate that. So I guess you'd better git."

James's face darkened to a livid red, fists bunched, but he was clearly outnumbered. Suddenly, he whirled toward Annalisa. She flinched but stood her ground, staring him down. Pride shot through Austin. She wasn't afraid anymore.

James gave her a sour look and wiped his hands together as if brushing her off. "I don't know why I bothered. If you choose this bunch of redneck losers over all I've done for you, you can all rot."

Sputtering invectives, James spun on his shiny loafers and stormed out of the Iron Horse.

Sweet relief rushed over Austin. His shoulders sagged. He closed his eyes as emotion surged through his bloodstream faster than white water rapids. Finally, Annalisa was rid of James Winchell, and he doubted she'd ever hear from the man again. Regardless of his own future in Whisper Falls, Austin had followed his conscience and kept her safe. No matter what it cost him, she was worth the price.

Even though he knew he should walk out now and not look back, he couldn't. Not without one last look at the woman who'd brought him back to life.

"Austin," she breathed.

His pulse skittered, stopped, then started again.

What he saw in her eyes nearly brought him to his knees. Not loathing. Not shame. Not even fear.

She came toward him, holding his gaze as if daring him to look away.

His heart, already in overdrive, revved up another notch.

"Are you okay?" he whispered, not caring that his voice shook.

She walked into his chest and wrapped her arms around his back. And her words humbled him. "I am now."

Was it possible?

Around them, the room had grown oddly silent. He heard a scrape of shoes, the bump of a metal implement against the tile. Then the world disappeared and all he could see and hear was the woman he loved, gazing up at him as if he was some kind of hero.

"But I thought—" he started, the scent of her hair in his nostrils was the fragrance of hope.

Her lips against his ear sent shudders down his spine. "You thought I wouldn't care about you because of something you didn't do? Could never have done?"

He shook his head, stunned and disbelieving. "Aren't you afraid? Aren't you worried I might be guilty, that I might hurt you, too?"

She pulled away a little so that he could see the sincerity in her expression. Blue eyes searched his. "After what you just endured for my sake?" Tenderly, she touched his cheek. "A man who let his most painful secret be broadcast to protect *me* is a man to respect and admire, not to fear. You didn't do those things James accused you of."

He stroked her golden hair, gazed into her sweet, beautiful face and hoped he wasn't dreaming. "You believe me."

"Of course I do. I know you, Austin Blackwell. You're a protector, a giver, not a taker. Thanks to you and Cassie and this wonderful little town, I've learned some very important things."

"What kinds of things?" Hardly able to believe this was happening, he rested his hands lightly at her waist, reveling in her sweet words.

"About myself, about faith and trust and love."

His heart knocked hard. "Love?"

She tiptoed up, kissed his chin. "Yes, love."

He drank her in, awed by the changes in her and in himself. The frightened, jumpy, broken person he'd met that day beneath Whisper Falls was gone. She was a different woman, just as he was a different man. Because of love.

And yet, love wasn't enough to save him.

Annalisa claimed to trust him, to love him, but what about this town now that they knew the truth about Austin Blackwell?

He let his hands drop from her waist, wishing

he could stay and be the man he saw in her eyes. But he wouldn't live under suspicion again.

"I can't live in Whisper Falls any longer."

She blinked, lips falling open in question. Oh, how he wished to kiss those lips and ignore the Pandora's box James had opened.

"I don't understand," she said.

"I'm a marked man, Annalisa. My past is public knowledge. You may believe I'm innocent, but not everyone will. I'll have to sell the ranch, move on." Again. The notion tore at his belly and left him bleeding.

Suddenly, a meaty hand clamped down on his shoulder. He'd almost forgotten they weren't alone.

"What are you talking about, boy?" Uncle Digger demanded, white eyebrows burrowed deep above his nose.

Austin was willing to face the truth on his own. He couldn't stay in Whisper Falls and be the object of stares and suspicions, but he could act like a man when he left.

Annalisa inched closer. She laced her fingers with his and held tight.

"You heard Winchell. People think I murdered my wife."

"Did you?"

"No!"

A slow smile quivered beneath Uncle Digger's

mustache. "I know it. So does everyone else in this room. Just figured you'd feel better if you said it out loud." He leaned his shovel against a table. "Rumors don't make a man, son."

"They weren't just rumors. I was arrested. Charged." His house ransacked and his DNA taken.

Creed Carter, owner of the annoying helicopter, stepped up beside Uncle Digger. "None of that made you guilty, did it?"

He shook his head. "No. I would never..."

Davis Turner slapped him on the shoulder. "We know that, Austin. We know you."

Austin couldn't take it in. He looked from one face to the next, saw nothing but acceptance and was awed to think this amazing group of people understood what the town that had known him all his life hadn't. He was not the kind of man to hurt a woman.

"The way I see it," Uncle Digger said, "you got derailed for a while, but you're back on track now. The Word says a man is like a tree, known by the fruit he bears. You helped out our sweet little Annalisa here."

"And you put up with me," Cassie said. "Everyone in this room knows how you put me back together when Darrell died."

"And you fulfilled my boy's dream of riding horses." This from Davis Turner.

"That was nothing."

"It is to him."

"You're bearing some mighty good fruit, son." Uncle Digger relocated his coal shovel against the counter. It was then Austin noticed the varmit gun lying across the counter. Thank goodness it had not come to that. "I think I speak for this group of your friends when I say we'd sure like you to stay in Whisper Falls and be part of us from now on. What do the rest of you think?"

Austin stared around at the assembled group, amazed and humbled by the nods and smiles of agreement. Terms like *one of our own* and *friend* filled the spot inside his chest that had been empty since the day Blair died.

Annalisa tugged at his hand. "See? They love you, too."

He gulped back the wad of emotion. "I don't know what to say."

She entwined her slender arms around his neck.

"Don't say anything, you dumb cowboy." Cassie stalked toward them, hair straightener raised in mock threat. "Kiss her. I'm tired of waiting."

Laughter trickled around the room. These were his friends, his neighbors, and here in his arms was his love.

Filled with wonder and lost in a pair of sky-blue eyes, Austin smiled down at his beloved and gave them what they asked for.

Epilogue

Spring comes to the Ozarks in a sudden burst of blooms and green. A profusion of wild plum and blushing cherry splash the roadsides with colorful blossoms before the vibrant redbud shows his handsome plumage. Their sweet scents mix and mesh, sending bees into a feeding frenzy and humans out into the fresh spring air.

On this particular afternoon, Annalisa drove the winding road to Austin's ranch, admiring spring's rebirth. In the past few months, she'd experienced a rebirth of her own and she rejoiced at what God had done in her life.

Embracing the wind, she rolled down her window and breathed in the fragrance. Her hair flew back from her shoulders, the air cool and fresh on her face.

So much had happened since last fall. James had effectively disappeared from her worry list.

Thanks to her wonderful Whisper Falls friends, she'd found an apartment she could afford and she'd thrown herself into the town and church, giving back to the community that had embraced her with such vigor.

Most important of all was Austin. Her heart leaped to know he was waiting for her arrival.

Even though he'd been reluctant to see her move into her own place, he'd understood her need for time. Time to be her own boss. Time to sort the feelings of the past from those of the present.

She still worked at the Iron Horse, although she was now taking classes online in tourism and marketing to better assist Miss Evelyn. She might never be rich, but she would be happy.

The little compact car bumped down the driveway, bringing the ranch house closer by the second.

Met by two wagging, barking dogs, she pulled to a stop and hopped out. The back door of the house slammed open and Austin came striding across the porch in jeans and boots, his head bare, black hair gleaming in the sun.

Happiness ricocheted through Annalisa. "Miss Evelyn sent pie and cookies."

Austin made a beeline for her, ignoring the promise of delicious treats.

"I missed you," he said, bending for a quick kiss that curled her toes and made her blush.

"Same here." She hugged him close, breathing his outdoorsy scent and reveling in his steady, dependable strength.

"Ready to ride?" He motioned toward the corral where two horses, Cisco and Blaze, stood saddled and waiting.

Comfortable in jeans and the pair of riding boots he'd bought her for Christmas, Annalisa handed off the bag of snacks and drinks. "Ready when you are."

They fell into step across the yard and into the corral.

"I have a surprise for you."

"What kind of surprise?"

"A good one." He frowned. "I hope."

"Tell me."

He snorted. "Then it wouldn't be a surprise."

He attached their snack bag to his saddle and held Blaze while she mounted. Then they were off, making the climb toward Whisper Falls. They took their time, happy just to be together as they talked and shared. She'd learned a great deal about her cowboy in the past few months, and yet each day with him was a discovery. He was deep and good, kind and sensible, but he still didn't like tourists traipsing over his pasture land. She supposed he never would.

Yet, with her as his hostess, he'd recently held a barbecue for their friends and had given horseback rides to the children. He was learning to trust again, to embrace people.

They reached the waterfall and dismounted on the woodsy trail. Mist rose from the foaming pool. The rush and roar of cascading water filled the air. Insects, fresh from a long winter nap, buzzed in the underbrush. Butterflies dipped and darted in a graceful dance on a profusion of wild blooms.

"This is a gorgeous place in spring," she said.

"I'm surprised no one else is up here today."

"Me, too." She slipped her hand into his. "But I'm glad. I wanted us to be alone. As if we're the only two people on earth. Us and God."

"I'll second that."

She looked up into his beloved face, heart full. "The rumor is true, you know."

He jacked an eyebrow. "What rumor?"

With a soft smile, she replied, "God does answer prayers beneath Whisper Falls. I know for sure because He answered mine. That awful day last fall? I asked God to protect me. I asked Him for help. I asked Him to show me the way to change my messed-up life." She sighed. "And He sent you."

Austin was silent for a long moment, his gaze focused somewhere behind her. Above them, puffy white clouds smiled benevolently from a pale blue sky. The waterfall splashed and sang with childlike glee.

Then suddenly, Austin was gone, scrambling over slick wet rocks down the rocky embankment that led to the secret "room" behind Whisper Falls. Annalisa cocked her head, puzzled at his odd behavior, and then with a shouted laugh, followed in pursuit.

She found him there, behind the falls in the very spot where she'd first laid eyes on him. That day, she'd been the one with a prayer on her lips. Today, Austin's head was down, his black hair sparkling with moisture drops, eyes closed in prayer. Annalisa's soul leaped for joy, knowing that he, like her, had found his way back to God, the great Lord of all who had gently wooed both of his broken children and brought them together in this place of healing.

With reverence and love she waited until Austin raised his head, spiky black lashes wet with mist. He reached for her, pulled her close, and even though dampness seeped through her clothes, she was warm from the inside out.

"I love you," he said.

"I know." And that was the beauty of real love that she'd never before understood. She knew he loved her. She had no doubts, no fears. Austin Blackwell loved her with everything in him. Her heart was safe with him. "And I love you, too, with all my heart."

His smile was gentle as he repeated her words. "I know."

His arms went around her as he rested his chin on her hair. She felt the dampness of his shirt, the heat of his skin. His chest rose and fell as a satisfied sigh slipped from his lips.

"This is the place we began," he said.

"Bad memories turned to good."

"That's God's way."

She smiled a little at the remark he would not have made last fall. They were standing close, a necessity on the narrow cliff ledge, but Annalisa thought she could never get close enough to her Ozark Mountain cowboy. "We've come a long way in a few months."

"Are you happy?"

"I couldn't be happier."

"I could be," he said, and the statement had her pulling away to stare at him in bewilderment.

"How?"

"If you'd marry me and have my babies. If you'd live with me up here in the mountains and be my forever love." He pulled in a long draft of air. "Marry me, Annalisa. Soon. I'm only half without you."

The smile budding in her heart burst into full bloom on her lips. She placed a hand on each side of his jaw, the manly roughness a thrill to her senses. "I thought you'd never ask."

He kissed her then, a seal of the promise made and a reminder of the passion to come.

Love, at last. The long drought of self-denial ended here and now. Or maybe it had ended last fall, on the day a cowboy chased a stray into the woods.

When the kiss ended, a soft rumble started in Austin's chest and rose to his throat in a bubble of laughter. He tilted his head toward Heaven.

"Thank You, Lord."

Annalisa's heart filled with gratitude. God had brought them both so far.

"You changed my life, Annalisa. You and the Lord. You brought me back to this place of understanding. I thought God had forsaken me, but He hadn't. He brought me here to heal and to find my way again."

"What did you pray for just now?" Annalisa whispered.

His rancher-rough fingers stroked her cheek, an innocently sensual touch that made her shiver. "I prayed that you'd say yes, and that I can be the man you need."

His words touched her to the soul. "You are. You always have been. God simply had to bring us here for us to understand."

"He really does answer prayer."

"No matter where it's prayed."

"And I think," Austin said with a mysterious

pump of his eyebrows, "he is about to answer another. Come on, surprise time."

"But I thought the proposal, here under the waterfall, was my surprise."

"Only the first." He gave her a tentative grin. "I hope you like the second one, too."

Fidgety, he gazed out beyond the waterfall to the woods. He was nervous, although she had no idea why.

Puzzled but willing to follow him anywhere, she took his outstretched hand. They climbed up the embankment. Austin kept one hand firmly at her waist, holding her close as their boots slipped and skidded on the way to higher ground. She never doubted he would keep her safe. Here and forever.

She could feel his excitement growing as he hurried her onward through the dense woods and upward to the riverbank overlooking Whisper Falls. Her curiosity grew. Being his wife was everything she'd dreamed of. What other wonderful surprise could he have for her?

"There," he said, voice smug.

As they burst through the underbrush, Annalisa's heart rocketed into overdrive. "Who—"

"Go on. See for yourself."

But she knew. With a cry of gladness, she broke into a run. "Olivia, Olivia!"

Her sister met her halfway, running, sobbing, laughing as they fell on each other.

"I'm sorry. I love you. I missed you. I was wrong."

"Me, too. Nothing is worth losing you."

They cried and forgave, laughed and adored.

After the storm of joy receded and the sisters stood, arms around each other's waists, faces red with tears, Annalisa pulled her cowboy into the circle of family.

He'd done this. For her.

"I love you," she said to him. "Thank you."

He looked so happy for her, and she knew he was. That was the beauty of Austin's love. Sacrificial and pure, a love that put her first. A scripture flashed through her head. *Husbands ought to love their wives as their own bodies.*

Austin would be that kind of husband because he was that kind of man.

She thought of that first time here at Whisper Falls, when she'd been alone and in danger. She thanked God that He had sent this man. A cowboy in search of a stray had discovered instead a stray heart, lost and broken and afraid.

And everything had changed, all because of a whispered prayer.

* * * * *

*Rita® Award–winning author
Linda Goodnight's new miniseries,
WHISPER FALLS,
is just getting started.
Don't miss more books set in this
heartwarming Ozark town later in 2013.
Look for them wherever
Love Inspired books are sold!*

Dear Reader,

Creating a new town and a new cast of characters for my new series, Whisper Falls, has been both fun and challenging. In *Rancher's Refuge,* you've met Uncle Digger, Miss Evelyn and a few other residents of the warm, quirky Ozark town. Most significantly, you met Austin and Annalisa, two wounded souls in need of God's direction and each other.

Healing and restoration are common themes in my books and *Rancher's Refuge* is no different. I don't intentionally choose those themes, but they seem to be the message God wants me to share. I think many around us are like Austin, functional and productive but hiding hurts deep inside, aching to be restored. Yet, our loving God doesn't want to leave us in that condition. He promises to be our refuge and our healer.

Thank you for reading. I hope you've enjoyed your visit to Whisper Falls and will come back again soon.

Sincerely,

Linda Goodnight

Questions for Discussion

1. Who was your favorite character in *Rancher's Refuge?* Why? Describe his or her personality.

2. Discuss how Annalisa's family relationships affected her as an adult. Which of the relationships do you think were most significant?

3. Describe the setting of this book. In what ways does the setting enhance the story?

4. How did Austin and Annalisa meet? What is Austin's first impression of her? What is her first impression of him? How was each right? How was each one wrong?

5. Austin believed God had let him down. Why? Have you ever felt this way? Was it true? How did you deal with it?

6. What was Austin's major conflict? What did he fear most and how did this affect his relationship with Annalisa? With other people in the town? With himself?

7. What is Annalisa's conflict? How did she get into such a dilemma?

8. Why does Austin choose to help Annalisa against his better judgment?

9. Who was Blair? How did she influence the story?

10. As a reader, did you guess what had happened to Blair? What were the clues that led to your conclusions?

11. What is the "rumor" about Whisper Falls? How did it get started and why? Was it wrong of the townspeople to use the story in this way?

12. Why was Annalisa estranged from her sister?

13. Describe the climax of this story. Did you find it effective? Why or why not?

14. Austin makes a sacrifice to protect Annalisa. What was it? How did you feel about his willingness to do such a thing?

15. Is there anything in this book that you can personally relate to? What is it and why?

LARGER-PRINT BOOKS!

GET 2 FREE LARGER-PRINT NOVELS PLUS 2 FREE MYSTERY GIFTS

Love Inspired

Larger-print novels are now available...

ReaderService.com

Manage your account online!

- Review your order history
- Manage your payments
- Update your address

*We've designed
the Reader Service website
just for you.*

Enjoy all the features!

- Reader excerpts from any series
- Respond to mailings and special monthly offers
- Discover new series available to you
- Browse the Bonus Bucks catalogue
- Share your feedback

Visit us at:

ReaderService.com